JOHNNY HAVOC

JOHNNY HAVOC

John Jakes began his career as a writer penning mysteries before turning to the historical novels, such as *North and South* and *California Gold,* upon which his popular reputation rests.

Johnny Havoc is the first of four adventures featuring the diminutive private investigator with flaming red hair. It was published as a paperback original by Belmont in 1960.

In this slam–bang adventure, Johnny's typical evening entertainment of picking up dolls in jazz bars is interrupted when he becomes embroiled in the murder of two honeymooners. Johnny dodges blondes and bullets without losing his wise-cracking good humor in this sharp and funny tale.

This edition, with a new introduction by the author, marks its first appearance in hardcover.

JOHNNY HAVOC

JOHN JAKES

THE
ARMCHAIR
DETECTIVE
LIBRARY

Introduction copyright © 1990 by John Jakes

Copyright © 1960 by John Jakes

First Armchair Detective Library Edition: March 1990

5 4 3 2 1

The Armchair Detective Library
129 West 56th Street
New York, NY 10019-3881

Library of Congress Cataloging-in-Publication Data

Jakes, John, 1932—
Johnny Havoc/John Jakes. —1st Armchair Detective Library ed.
p. cm.
ISBN 0-922890-20-X (trade ed.)
ISBN 0-922890-18-8 : (collectors ed.) $25.00.
ISBN 0-922890-19-6 (lim. ed.) : $75.00
I. Title
PS3560.A37J64   1990
813'.54—dc20   89-77790
CIP

Printed in Great Britain

INTRODUCTION

This novel and the three that followed it from Belmont Books, a long–vanished paperback house, are four of my favorite offspring. Writers often speak of their works as children, with reason. All are part of the writer's flesh, to be loved, cherished, and examined with growing curiosity, amazement—occasionally horror—as they grow older. Like children, sometimes their earlier promise, or the enthusiasm the writer felt for them, doesn't hold up. But the love of the parent usually persists.

So it is with this story about a 5'1" private eye with a fondness for Brooks Brothers clothes and (talk about dated) pork–pie hats. Memory refuses to tell me how I first conceived of the character, and the series (for years, I could never get beyond three or four books with series characters because the books began to sound the same to me, and writing boredom set in; it happened with Havoc, and also with a nice little sf cycle of related novels that I undertook for my friend Don Wollheim; I avoided the problem with *The Kent Family Chronicles* and *The North and South Trilogy* by shifting each succeeding novel into a new, intrinsically different historical period, each with its own interesting research challenge.

I do remember that, from the start, Havoc was short, thus unable to deal physically with novelistic menaces and goons, hence had to live by his wits and his lip. He quickly evolved to my Champion of All the Short People Everywhere, because he always out-talked, out-thought, and outwitted the baddies. I am 6′1″, but I liked that. Maybe that's why I still like him.

My agent at the time, Scott Meredith, didn't have much luck marketing this first Havoc novel. Perhaps it was too offbeat. Perhaps it was too slapstick (there was always to be one chase sequence in the book, *a lá* the Keystone Kops). Or perhaps it was just too imperfect. But Meredith was always dogged, circulating scripts until they almost literally fell apart. He found a couple of editors at newly-organized Belmont Books who liked the character and the story. Belmont changed my original title, *Here Comes Havoc*, to *Johnny Havoc*, but otherwise presented the work exactly as I'd written it, without editorial changes.

Over the years, in letters and personal conversations, quite a few readers and colleagues have told me that they remember Havoc and the canon with a good deal of fondness. Imagine my feelings, then, when my friend and fellow member of Mystery Writers of America, Otto Penzler, phoned me one sunny afternoon last fall to tell me his plan to reprint the early crime novels of a number of writers, including yours truly, if I'd be willing to see J. Havoc's adventures in print again.

You're holding the result of my enthusiastic response.

I hope you'll like this kid of mine. He's thirty years older than he was when he first popped into the world. He isn't perfect; but as noted above, I still have a lot of affection for him. I'm grateful to Otto and his newest imprint for giving J.H. a second lease on life.

John Jakes
Hilton Head Island, South Carolina, January 1990

JOHNNY HAVOC

Chapter 1

I WAS SITTING with this lovely little doll in the grape-colored lighting of the cellar nightclub known as The Ego, soaking up Scotch and listening to Flying Henry Washington and his group blow out their collective brains.

The doll was a redhead with gobs of class. Furthermore, she was just five feet high. I hadn't met a decent doll my size in months.

Have you ever considered the problems facing a party who stands a mere five feet one inch? Exactly how many females of that height or under do you suppose reside in a city of several million souls? Further, how many of these dolls are worth looking at a second time? If you locate a desirable item, it's sheer folly to let it escape for even an instant.

So I sat, soaking up Scotches and growing soggier every minute, fearful that if I left she'd melt or vanish. But finally Nature's Call made like a distant tidal wave.

"Excuse me, Charlene," I announced, getting up and tripping on the chair. "Be right back."

Lurching and stumbling, I made my way to my haven.

When I emerged and lit a cigarette, they were waiting for me.

They came forward out of the shadows and a large picture of the Eiffel Tower. One of them boxed me on the left, another on the right. Distantly Flying Henry's vibes belled and rang. I looked from one to the other, my stomach screwing up tight. They had unfriendly expressions and wore credit clothing.

The angel of mercy on my left was tall, well over six feet, with sunken cheeks and a reddish hick jaw. I found myself

5

staring at his tie clasp, which had the virtue of being feature-
less, unlike his lantern face which had a mean kind of delight
on it. His comrade on my right, slightly under six feet, carried
an immense corporation and had kangaroo pouches of
blubber beneath his eyes. Upon his tie I noted a hand-painted
view of the sea labelled Biscayne Bay. He also had a deep
tan. A couple of friendlier fellows you wouldn't want to
meet, especially since Tall had his hand in his side pocket
while Fat, the bolder of the two, came right out in the open
and jammed his heater up against my larynx. *Plong plong*,
went the vibes. They had me.

"Excuse me," I said. "There's probably been a mistake."

"Took the midget long enough to go to the head, didn't it?"
Tall inquired of Fat.

"We thought you were going to sit in there all night,"
remarked Fat.

"Look, guys, I think you've located the wrong party. My
name is Havoc."

"That's right," said Tall. "We know it's Havoc. There's no
mistake."

"We'd like you to step through that door at the end of the
hall, so we could have a little chat with you," announced
Fat, self-consciously adjusting the view of Biscayne Bay and
settling his tropical hat on his head, using the hand which did
not press a weapon against my voice-box. "We been sloshing
up crappy liquor for two hours, just waiting for you to cut
yourself free from that little broad. You might say we're in
something of a rush. You might also say that arguing with us
would invite disaster."

"Miami Joe is very emotional, midget," remarked Tall.
"He can't stand having his wishes refused. In fact, you'd be
a fool to refuse them, midget. Now, if you stood about my
size . . ." Tall finished the sentence with a snicker. While
one segment of my soul burned, another quavered. They had
me cold, the way overgrown punks can always get you cold
when they're holding a foot and a half of extra size and a
cannon over your head.

"Care to move along, little lad?" said Miami Joe, goug-
ing my voice-box once again.

Allowing my natural cowardice free reign, I nodded my head. Miami Joe stood aside, motioning with his rod-muzzle. At the end of the poster-bedecked and totally empty corridor —was I the only guy in the whole damned joint who had to go to the can, ever?—stood a green-painted iron door. Through this they directed me, into an alley leading behind the club. A tomcat yowled atop an ashcan. Tall gave it a boot and sent it flying, chuckling low. Oh, they were a pair of dandies. For no reason at all I began to whistle *Going Home*, until Miami Joe pasted me in the chops with the back of his hand.

"Keep your trap fastened, little lad," he growled, ramming me against a brick wall.

"Now," announced Tall with a sigh. "Now tell us where a certain friend of yours can be found. Tell us where Lorenzo Hunter and his wife went on their honeymoon."

"What makes you think I know anybody named Lorenzo Hun—"

Whap.

My head conked the brick wall. It had been the wrong thing to say, I reasoned while recovering consciousness. Tall leaned close to me, leering, scowling, pouring forth a string of references to my size and parentage which would cause the post office to revoke mailing privileges. Fortunately, Tall's excess of temper caused the usually emotional Miami Joe to gain control of the situation, and he tugged his comrade back with a growl.

"Not yet, Ed. He can't tell us anything if we kick all his teeth out."

"I'll kick his teeth out if he doesn't open up, the snivelling little wart."

"Hear that?" Miami Joe said, scowling darkly. "I'm not the only one gets hot under the collar when things go wrong. Ed here's got a temper like a stick of dynamite. Slow fuse, but once it burns down—Bammo!" He conjured all sorts of visions of mayhem in the empty ring dark. Didn't anybody ever walk down alleys any more? Miami Joe went on, "I'll give you a break, little lad. I'll spend a couple of seconds telling you what we know, so you haven't got any excuse to stall us. Item one—"

He puncuated the recitation by various pokes to my throat and cheek region with the muzzle of his weapon.

"Your name is indeed John Havoc. You apparently are a bum, since you don't have a job. You sit around all the time in highclass joints like Twenty-Two. The kids in blue know who you are. They keep an eye on you. See? Haven't we got the whole thing down?"

"You fascinate me. Like a couple of cobras."

Well, they let me have it a few more times, Miami Joe growing just as unsteady and emotionally aroused as his gangling friend Edward. I wondered whether Flying Henry Washington and his entourage would take a break at set's end and step in the alley for a smoke. Probably never ever. Probably they had given up smoking and decided to play on all night. Tall Edward did a few things to my ears with his long fingers. It was pretty humiliating.

I decided them, penciling them down in my private skull notebook, that if I ever got shed of them, I'd do my best to settle a score or two. But frankly, it didn't look like I was going to get shed, unless the mortician and his staff carried me away.

"Item two," Miami Joe panted, huffing like a bellows. "You number among your friends and-or acquaintances a seedy Tennessean named Lorenzo Hunter. Go on, give us the innocent stare all you want. Hunter plays guitar in the band at The French Quarter. Or he did until today. He got married this morning at City Hall. And you stood up for him. Now, our question, little lad, is just this. Where did Lorenzo Hunter and that Magruder dish he married go for their post-nuptials? Where'd they go for their honeymoon?"

"Let me explain something, gang. Very quickly and finally."

"Do you know where they went, pin-head?" announced tall Ed, with a loss of patience.

I raised my hands in an attempt to placate them. "Let me explain."

"Let him explain," mimicked Miami Joe in piping tones.

"Old Lorenzo Hunter's what you'd call an acquaintance, not a friend. I hang around The French Quarter now and then. I met him once or twice. I don't believe the guy has two real friends in the world. When he asked me to stand up for him at the wedding, he as much as said he didn't have any close friends to call on. He just needed a witness. I don't mind doing a guy a good turn, even if he isn't my sworn brother. So I went down to City Hall . . ."

Now came the difficult part. The foregoing had been truth, but what was coming was pure balderdash: ". . . and I signed a paper and stood there while he married the Magruder girl, period. I wasn't a best man in the strict sense, guys. Not to the point of having the keys to his car in my pocket and a road map concealed in my trust. No, Lorenzo handled that part himself. He didn't tell me, I didn't ask. So if you want to know where Lorenzo is spending his bridal night, you'll have to seek out another oracle." I tried to put a winning smile upon my face; I wanted to get shed of them in the worst way so I could think up something to fix them for keeping me away from Charlene. The winning smile didn't win anything except a booby prize consisting of another clout out of tall Edward.

"Midget, tell one more lie and you're as good as interred."

"You must have had a good education, to use such big wor—"

Whap, whap. Mouthy me.

The bellows-like frenzy of Miami Joe's stentorian breathing laved me in aromas of yesterday's toothpaste. He bent the lapels of my two-hundred-dollar Brooks Brothers suit into all sorts of unsightly shapes. He bounced the rear of my head against the brick wall a few additional times.

"Perhaps we have not made it crystal clear, little lad. We are not a couple of fun-loving kids on a picnic. We are serious. There's a hundred grand wrapped up in this affair, and a nice fat place for a couple of legit businessmen like us to make a sum of money in the good, old, respectable pharma . . . pharma . . ."

"Pharmaceutical," interrupted the scholarly Edward.

". . . yeah, pharmaceutical racket. If we are playing games, little lad, it's kick the can, and your head is the can. We just won't stand here and have you tell us no, no, no. We'll do a little something to loosen up your tongue. For a hundred grand you think your crummy Dale Carnegie grin is going to send us off saying sorry we bothered you? In other words, I want you to get this point exceedingly straight. We do not accept an answer of no, I don't know. That kind of answer is going to put you in the charity ward of the hospital."

"You're growing emotional," I said, wriggling to release my lapels.

"Where'd they go, little lad?" questioned Miami Joe, blashing my jaw with his weapon.

"I tell you, friends, I couldn't possibly tell you, because I don't—"

"Ah, for Christ's sake," exclaimed tall Edward in dolorous tones, "let's quit talking."

So they did.

When you stand five feet one and they have you cold, you can fight but it doesn't do a great deal of good. They bounced me between them, knocking all the sense out of me, repeating their question about Lorenzo Hunter's honeymoon hideaway. I knew. Oh, I knew, all right. But I'd be damned if I'd tell them.

Back and forth along the alley I went, their kick-the-can container, until suddenly they dropped me cold on the bricks. I told them for the final time I simply had no idea where Lorenzo Hunter and the ex-Shirley Magruder had closeted themselves for their first night's romp, but as they deposited me unceremoniously on the floor of the alley, I assumed dimly they no longer cared. A steel door clanged. Voices were raised hilariously.

"No, kids, I couldn't tell you where they went," I said to a brick an eighth of an inch under my nose. The voices stopped. Something went pop-hiss. So Flying Henry's group craved a smoke at last, I thought. I turned over, raised my head, sat up, looked around, groaned, smiled, and passed out.

Chapter 2

AFTER AN EXCRUCIATING period of dizziness, I regained my senses and was lifted up by Flying Henry and a number of way-out plaid-coated music-makers. Flying Henry himself was a citizen of uncertain age, the most conservative guesses placing him at eighty-seven. A thatch of short snowy hair contrasted with the shining ebony of a face lighted by gleams from the open corridor of the club.

"Earl, you fetch Johnny a shot of booze," I heard him say as he adjusted my shoulders against the brick wall with all the tenderness of a doting mother. "Here, boy." He pressed his spotless white handkerchief into my hands. "Wipe up all that catsup around your mouth. What happened? It can't be drink. You're not the kind who gets falling-down blind, I know that much. You got trouble, John boy?"

"I think so, Henry. I was a contestant in a quiz. I lost."

"Here," said the helpful Earl, returning with an old-fashioned glass loaded brim-high with what I smelled to be the finest of Chivas Regal's factory output. One mellow flaming sip of the hootch restored me somewhat and improved my flagging vitamin balance. With Earl's assistance I stood and lit a smoke. Flying Henry and his small crew all had expressions of the greatest sympathy on their faces. Fat help.

"Care to talk about the encounter?" asked Flying Henry tactfully. As though preparing for something distasteful, he swallowed deep. "Should we, ah, call police?"

"Perish the thought," replied I. "I stay as far from them as necessary. No, this is something private. Though what, exactly, I can't tell."

In my clarifying brain, however, little cash registers had begun to tinkle in a most insinuating manner. A hundred thousand dollars? The pharmaceutical business? What was it all about? Besides money. Of which I never had enough.

I grew aware of Flying Henry and his retinue hanging on my every word. To satisfy them I asked: "Hey, what about

11

that little chick at my table? Charlene. Any of you boys see
her? Is she still—"

As though a friend had passed to his reward, Flying Henry
shook his head. "Gone."

"Hell's fire. All right. Pass me that booze container once
again, kindly. Ah. Thanks. Now another question, gents. Did
any of you see a pair of mopes hanging around the place
tonight? One very tall, with a reddish jaw? Called Ed. The
other was a big tub of lard with a sun-lamp burn and a
picture of Miami painted on his tie. Surprisingly enough he
went by the name of Miami Joe. I've never heard of them."
I squinted. "Flying Henry, if you or your boys know them,
I'd appreciate your telling me. I don't want to forget those
two sweethearts, not ever. Unless of course they happen to
be boon companions—"

"Not by a damn sight," spoke the group's drummer man
in a growl. "I know them."

"Personally, Alvin?" inquired Flying Henry.

"No, thank you. The tall one is Sparks, Ed Sparks. The
other is Miami Joe Jalasca. As far as I know, they're still
working for Charlie Cain. Doing what, I don't know. But
either one is a bad bet. The both of them together are worse
than Champagne Music."

Puzzle pieces dropped in place in my slightly clanging
head. "Charlie Cain? You mean Candy Cain, Alvin? The
hood who runs around with a bag of peppermints in his
pocket?"

"He doesn't mean Buffalo Bill Rappaport," answered
Flying Henry with a rueful expression. "John, my friend, if
you have difficulties with Candy Cain, I would first of all
settle them peacefully. Secondly, don't underestimate him.
Or sneer at him, either. He's not a big-timer. Doesn't have
the class or the brains to know how to juggle cost-accounting
figures and income tax returns like the top dogs. Never
made it up the social ladder, if you know what I mean.
On the other hand, he's no side-street wallet-mugger. Medium-time, I suppose you might call him. The worst kind
around. Mad he can't move with the upper crust, determined

not to mix with the trash. Do almost anything to stay where he is."

"I saw him in Twenty-Two once," I remembered dimly. "They threw him out when he started lobbing his peppermints at some broad at another table. Liquored pretty high. He broke a couple of noses before they managed to eject him."

"Have no truck with him," was Flying Henry's sage advice.

I, however, couldn't resign myself to the peaceful road he suggested. I re-arranged my expensive wardrobe, picked at a few blood drops which had damaged its fabric, and prepared to depart.

"Thanks a lot, Flying Henry. You, too, boys." I extended my hand. "I'll be moving."

"If you see any bags of peppermints on the sidewalk, don't pick them up," the old man said obliquely, a kindly light radiating off his face. There weren't many souls in the world who would give a hustler like me such a gaze of friendship.

Somewhat soothed and balmed, re-paid in a small way for the indignities banged down on me by Candy Cain's hired biceps, I bid farewell to the polite crew of plaid-suited musicians, walked out the alley, back in the front door of The Ego, retrieved my porkpie and went to pick up my convertible in the parking lot.

Mental cash-registers were zinging. A hundred grand? Pill business? As I drove through the warm night toward my wee little home in the high rent district, it occurred to me suddenly that Lorenzo Hunter's bride, the former Shirley Magruder, was connected to a pill works. In a moment I would remember the name of her father's plant across the river in the Industrial Flats. But Candy Cain hardly fit in, that I could see.

But then how did a gangling, shy, ex-con guitar player in the town's brassiest nitery fit with the likes of a girl such as Shirley Magruder? As I had told my buddies Sparks and Jalasca, I was not a good friend of Lorenza Hunter's. He had none that I knew about. I was a bar-mate, a fleeting ship passing him in the alcoholic night. Oh, Havoc, you poetic slob. But it was true.

The poor lout had obviously been at a loss for someone to lend his wedding a feeling of near-normalcy. I passed muster and indulged in one of my few acts of behavior which had no direct bearing on monetary profit. Why Lorenzo Hunter had married a broad like Shirley Magruder remained a mystery. True, the kid had a big build, nearly a forty-four, and Lorenzo was a lascivious old hound. But the ex-Miss Magruder spoke in a finishing-school twang, wore horn-rimmed glasses, and had a beak of a nose that made her look like a stuffed eagle. I suppose bemused Lorenzo never gazed above the neckline.

Reaching my dismally expensive lodgings on the fifth floor of a swanky street overlooking the bridge and the river, I took a hot bath to kill my aches. Then I turned out all the lights, put Flying Henry's album on the machine and settled down in my bathrobe in a basket chair by the window. I drank a Scotch or two.

It was none of my blamed business, was it?

Still, a hundred grand somewhere . . .

Mr. Havoc, that's your greed speaking.

Hell, yes it is, but what about the fact that Lorenzo Hunter might not know a nasty party like Candy Cain was looking for him? Could I overlook that?

Of course I could. Flying Henry had said . . .

But for God's sake, Mr. Havoc, a telephone call won't hurt. After all, he asked you to be in his wedding. He could have walked on the street and picked up just any old seedy floater.

That comparison stung somewhat. I solved the hurt by dialing Long Distance.

"Operator, I'd like to speak with Mr. Lorenzo Hunter at the Mohawk Mountain Lodge."

After various preliminaries I was finally connected with a nasal old soul of undetermined sex and age. Repeating my request, I was paid off with an immoral kind of titter.

"Sorry, there, feller. Mister Hunter told the desk he didn't

wish any disturbances of any kind, him being on a honeymoon and all. You git the point, don't you, feller?"

"I understand, Calvin, but it's very urgent that I talk
with him."

"The name is Oral, and don't get smart with me. There
ain't a blessed thing I can do, because he left everybody
orders not to bother him. If you want to talk to Mr. Sidgwick
the manager, why, I guess you can just go right over my
head, but I don't think you'll git very far. Mr. Sidgwick
says the guest is always right."

"That's pretty original."

"I think it is, too. You want me to ring Mr. Sidgwick?
Won't do no good—"

"I'm just an impetuous fool. Go ahead and ring him up,
old friend of my heart and soul."

I heard the guardian of the circuits and the lodge desk
mutter something to the effect of "Jesus Q. Christ, these
long-distance city types," but eventually I was connected
with Mr. Sidgwick himself. As Oral had gloomily predicted,
he was on the side of wedded love and the angels. Finally,
after ten minutes of gabbing, I convinced him that if he
rang the cottage in which Lorenzo Hunter and his bride
were quartered, Lorenzo would inevitably answer because
he'd know it was of vital importance. I wasn't sure whether
it was or not, but did not inform Mr. Sidgwick. When at
last he gave in, the cottage phone rang and rang, a hundred
and twenty seconds at least.

Mr. Sidgwick cut in again, pretty damned smugly, to tell
me jeeringly there was no answer. Apparently his guest Mr.
Hunter did not think anything could be sufficiently important
to draw him from the blissful embraces of his new-found
bride. It was pretty sickening.

"Guess that settles the hash, don't it, feller?" responded
the worthy Oral, cutting in on the line again. He couldn't
conceal his glee. "Sorry you wasted so much money just
gassin' and gittin' nowhere. But then you city boys can
afford to throw it around, I guess."

"Wait just a damned minute!" I yelled. "I've got to talk
with Hunter, even if it means you goofing it out to his

cottage and knocking on his door and getting him up from—"

"Feller," responded Oral in pitying tones, "I'm just going to have to cut off your water right now. I got no time to waste talking to loonies."

Click, we were out of business, and I was out of patience. When it came to basics, did the whole thing matter anyway?

Of course not.

What did I owe the lanky guitar-plunker?

Nothing at all. Right?

Absolutely correct.

Have another delicious jolt of Scotch booze, go to bed and forget it.

At fifteen minutes until five in the morning, not having slept a blessed instant during the night, I crawled into my convertible and drove up the Parkway seventy-nine miles to the Mohawk Mountain Lodge, cursing myself all the way.

I was sentimental, I was a sucker. I would never get rich doing things like this. But by God, once I hammered on the door and waked the blushing bridegroom, I'd swear never again to get myself entangled—

Then, suddenly, I realized I was getting myself entangled with the police.

I had been tooling up a long gravel road. After rounding a curve, I braked hard at the edge of a large parking lot bathed in early morning light. It was only a few minutes past seven in the morning. Birds were chirruping, which made me feel ghastly, it was all so unfamiliar. But I might have sworn I had driven into the heart of rush-hour traffic. The lot was messed with the most monstrous tangle of police and guest vehicles imaginable. My convertible was nearly smashed by an ambulance that went roaring by down the mountain.

Crowds of guests in curlpapers and pajama-and-lumber-jack-shirt outfits milled over the place. Officious authoritarian types in the uniform of sheriff's police strutted here and there, focusing their attention, it seemed, on a small green-shuttered cottage beside the rambling structure of the main lodge. I found a parking place and climbed out.

I adopted a somewhat craven manner and infiltrated the crowd. A beefy matron with spots of cold cream on her cheeks, a man's parka over her massive bosoms and an ivory cigarette holder in her mouth, had just turned away from a pair of companions. Although she gave me a suspicious glare as I approached, I took off my porkpie and inquired:

"Excuse me, madam. I'm a salesman on the road . . . new in this part of the country . . . driving all night . . . saw the sign on the highway down the hill . . . wanted to get a room . . . catch a little shuteye . . . doesn't appear I can get through . . . what's going on?"

"Murder, that's what," she explained, regarding me even more suspiciously.

"Who—I mean, where? Ah, is that right? You don't really mean murder!"

"Young man, I don't mean bar mitzvah," she replied with a snort. "I mean exactly what I said—murder."

A crocodile tear washed from her eye, down across the cleansing cream upon her cheek. "A pair of poor honeymooners. A youth and his bride, in that very cottage over there. A maid noticed one of the window panes broken when she started out to the supply cottage for her linens. She looked in the window and saw them, both shot, the poor things. I suppose you think I'm making this all up? Just a minute, I'll call Mr. Sidgwick. He's the lodge manager. He'll tell you it's all true, all sordid and true."

"No, madam," I said emptily. "Don't call the manager. I believe you."

One of the minions of the sheriff's police was stumping through the murmurous crowd, making menacing motions left and right with a billy. "All right, folks. Time to quit beating your gums and get back inside, there's nothing to see and we got work to do."

A tight feeling in my gut, I waited for him to approach. "Officer—?"

"Didn't you hear what I said to the rest of the people, shrimp? Move it out."

"Yeah, sure, right away. I just wondered whether you

could tell me approximately when the killing took place. I mean, it's rather important—"

"Rather important, huh? So you can sit around with the rest of these damned ghouls and munch over all the details? Sometime around one A.M., pal," he continued in a tired, sarcastic matter. "And if that satisfies all your little cravings, how about getting the hell out of the way so the police can do what you pay taxes for them to do?"

The fact that I hadn't paid any taxes in six years was hardly worth mentioning. As the crowd began to disperse, I ambled back to my convertible, sucking on a butt and attempting to reassure myself that I'd done all possible for Lorenzo Hunter. I had tried to telephone him somewhere near midnight, shortly after returning from The Ego. I couldn't possibly have driven from The Ego to the lodge between the time I picked myself up out of the alley and one o'clock in the morning. I don't like killing any better than the next guy but I'd done what I could for him. It hadn't been good enough, of course.

I had gotten less than a quarter of a mile down the hill toward the highway when I knew again what I had known for so many years:

Deep down, I was a lousy rat.

"Havoc," I said, "you are a sawed-off, no-good, hustling little rat." Every time I murmured it, my inner soul said leeringly: *A hundred thousand clams.*

Chapter 3

NO ONE REASONABLY sane and lacking business to conduct would ever go near Industrial Flats.

Even when the sun shone brightly on the city, noon was grimy gray across the river. Assorted iron works, soup factories, missile assembly plants, polystyrene brew-kitchens and children's toy manufacturing firms belched oddly-hued and strangely-scented smokes over whole square miles of land, all hours of the day. One of the largest of these tangles of pipe and junkwork, I discovered on approaching, was a mammoth establishment which blew out great colorless clouds of something which smelled of a mixture of ammonia and consommé. A wide bronze sign over the gate identified the factory as U.P.I.—UNITED PHARMACEUTICALS INCORPORATED.

A lizard-eyed guard in a brass-buttoned uniform waved me distrustfully to a parking area, even though he had telephoned to the grimy brick building at the end of the main quadrangle and found that a person named Havoc did indeed have an appointment with the leading light of the nostrum works, board chairman Thomas F. X. Magruder.

Two days had passed since the day of the double funeral. The stories in the newspapers of the dual chilling of Lorenzo Hunter and his bride had been starkly simple, without appreciable facts:

The pair had been killed with a silenced weapon of .38 caliber. No one on the hotel premises had heard the shots. A bartender who had just closed the lodge cocktail establishment and was on his way home thought he had seen a single figure leaving the cottage around twelve midnight, said figure climbing into a car whose make the bartender could not remember. The sheriff's police, of course, were following several leads. They always did. Straight to the unsolved file.

No relatives had claimed Lorenzo Hunter's corpse. Apparently he had none. According to the papers he had been interred at Shirley Magruder's family cemetery, but not within the limits of the family plot. That smacked of something, I didn't know what.

On the second floor of the U.P.I. administration building I was ushered into a panelled reception room and kept waiting in a chair by an old, sterile-looking maiden of withered proportions and visage. A thick oak door opened.

". . . and, damn it, you'd better have it out of the pilot plant by the first of August, or you can look for new jobs!" roared a husky voice. Several craven personages in white coats and trousers paraded out unhappily, carrying clip boards and other scientific-looking paraphernalia. The unloved virgin adjusted her spectacles and informed me I could enter.

Behind the five-hundred-dollar desk in the spacious sanctum sat a bull of a man in a gray pin-stripe with thinning hair to match. He had jowls and a dangerous, hard blue eye.

On the walls hung various photos of mystic-looking chemical equipment. Not a paper or smear of dust disturbed the gleaming desk top, from which Thomas F. X. Magruder's unfriendly face owled at me upside down. I noticed in a corner of the room a silent stock ticker; I assumed he had told it to shut up and it had. My porkpie in my hand, I introduced myself.

"Yes, I had our company librarian run a check on you, Havoc, after you telephoned yesterday for an appointment."

Palms down on the desk top, Mr. Magruder skewered me with those blue eyes as though I was poor butterfly nailed to the surface of a cigar box and ready to be treated with formaldehyde. "Frankly, I wasn't too pleased with what I read. You have had your name in the newspapers a few times during the past couple of years. Each time the escapade was, to say the least, unsavory."

"No one ever proved a thing!" I countered hotly.

"Young man, from what you told my secretary, you were a friend of Lorenzo Hunter and my step-daughter Shirley. That is sufficient recommendation for me—either to kick you downstairs or throw you out the window, whichever would do you the most harm. Now, what do you want? I've a meeting at eleven."

"I didn't know Miss Magruder was a step-daughter," I burbled, trying to unbalance him.

Deep in his well-tonsured jowls he made a rumbling noise again. "Well, then," he said with considerable acid, "you've learned something, haven't you? Yes, she was my step-daughter, my second wife's child by a previous marriage. I am twice a widower. I have just buried my step-daughter, Mr. Havoc. She was a little bitch. Perhaps if you wish to know anything more about my personal life, you should hire yourself to conduct an investigation. Isn't that your forte? That's what the clippings said. You sell yourself for all sorts of dubious assignments, none of which are covered by a legal license to practice as an investigator."

He pulled open a desk drawer, lifted out a clock, stared, put it back, slammed the drawer, then linked his fingers together on the desk top with a smug expression.

I reached out my toe, hooked one of his fancy chairs and dragged it toward me. I de-flowered his desk by hurling my porkpie on it and sat down. I began:

"Mr. Magruder, I think you have me correctly identified. As a matter of fact, I came here with the thought that we might do business in your hour of grief."

Old F. X. chuckled.

"I spotted you for a greedy little wretch the moment you waltzed in here. I like that. No man rises to the top by sucking his thumb in a corner. I was never particular about what I took, or from whom."

Down came his eyebrows, growling and vee-shaped. "On the other hand, you palm yourself off as a friend of that seedy guitar player Hunter, and I suppose you'll also tell me you were a soul-mate of Shirley's. I believe I made it clear I did not precisely care for my step-daughter. Taking life is shameful but my hour of grief, as you so tearfully put it, does not extend beyond that point."

"No, Mr. Magruder, I wasn't acquainted with your daughter. But a few nights ago I took some lumps from a couple of characters who mentioned a hundred thousand dollars and the pharmaceutical business. They were very interested in knowing the whereabouts of Hunter and Shirley. To the point of practically cracking me wide open to get me to tell them where the newlyweds had gone on their honeymoon." I leered. "Interested?"

From the vague, undecipherable flickers on F. X.'s map, I thought he was.

"Who were these persons, Mr. Havoc? You've aroused my curiosity."

"Why, F. X.," I said blandly, "would you show a hole card in a stud game?"

"Heh-heh."

It was a most unusual sound. It merely gurgled out of his throat, no changes of expression accompanying it.

"Heh-heh. Yes, you are a greedy wretch, indeed. It must

have something to do with your height. Oh, no offense meant. All right, Havoc. I'll show you one of the cards in my hand. Was one of the people to whom you referred a young, wishy-haired man? Extremely pale, bookish-looking, glasses? What you might describe as a scientific sort?" He paused. "A fink?"

"No, sir. The gentlemen were finks, but hardly scientific. These kids play nasty. They're looking for easy bucks."

"The pot calls the kettle," remarked F. X. with a smirk.

"All the same, they're some way connected with your business, your step-daughter and a hundred thousand. I don't know what the connection is. But with these characters interested, you may be in for some unsavory trouble. Possibly for some kind of real jam."

I let it out in a rush. "Obviously, I'm fishing, Mr. Magruder. But if you have trouble, I think we could work out a deal. For five thousand retainer and an additional five thousand on completion of an assigned task, you can buy my services."

"My God!" cried the board chairman. "You're brazen and insufferable! Why do you think UPI contracts yearly for over one hundred thousand dollars' worth of work from the Sturns Agency? Because when we need special help, we know that the biggest detective firm in the country can do a job."

I shrugged and lit up a smoke.

"So throw away the cash, F. X. All I'm saying is, some bad people see cash to be made. It's hooked to your daughter. Maybe you can tell me how. If you think the Sturns creeps can get into the kind of places I can, why, you're not a very good judge of character after all."

He sucked in a deep, long breath. "Mr. Havoc, you are something of a madman yourself."

"It takes that kind to do the sort of jobs I do, F. X. Shall I exit and let you phone your wet nurses at Sturns, or have we something we can discuss?"

"One minute."

Magruder pressed an ivory button on his desk, opened a

drawer, bent his head and appeared to be speaking to an invisible box.

"Miss Zif, have there been any new reports from Sturns or that county crew upstate concerning the whereabouts of Dr. Willis? No? Very well. No, blast it, I haven't forgotten the meeting. They'll just have to play with their flipcharts a little while longer."

Slamming the drawer, he tented his fingers again. "Havoc, you have planted some extremely disturbing thoughts in my head. Until a moment ago I was ready to heave you out of here. Now I don't think I will. Ten thousand dollars taken from the till will make old Fuddleson the treasurer scream like he's been emasculated. On the other hand, with Nirvana there's a twenty-million-dollar market at stake. Chancing ten thousand on a crackbrain such as you is peanuts, Havoc!"

I coughed discreetly. "Beg pardon, F. X., but you've left me somewhere south of the hind end of this whole conversation. Who would this Dr. Willis be? And you mentioned something about Nirvana. It's all pretty esoteric. You'll have to bring yourself down to more concrete terms if you expect me to be any help. Otherwise let the Sturns mopes handle it."

Somewhat miffed by my impertinence, Magruder blew out a few ruffled bass-note coughs and replied caustically, "I was not speaking of the state of nirvana, Havoc, which you would doubtlessly equate with a perpetual string of suckers pouring cash into your open pockets."

Determined to jeopardize my monetary health no further, I let the barb fly on beyond me as the venerable chairman announced, "No, when I speak of Nirvana, I spell it with a capital letter. That is the name chosen by our marketing panel for a new tranquilizing compound discovered in the UPI labs. Believe me, Havoc, it's going to revolutionize the neuro-psychiatric market, if those sneaky bastards in South Bend don't beat us to it. Never mind. I'll come back to that. It may be connected."

His hard blue eye went a-roving, a-musing, and I went a-wondering to what illegitimate inhabitants of South Bend he referred. But then, in big business, the giants carve out their own devious paths. I puffed on a smoke and let him take his own sweet muddling time. After all, for ten thousand clams.

"Do you recall the pale, wispy gentleman whom I called fink a few moments ago?"

"Clearly, F. X. This wouldn't be Dr. Willis, would it? He sounds doctorish."

"And he is. One of the really crack brains in our chemistry section. A group leader. Responsible for some of UPI's most financially successful products."

"I gathered from your conversation with your secretary that he's vanished, eh?"

"He has, he has," F. X. answered with a grimace of distaste. "Willis had been looking bad lately, very bad. He thought he was in love with my step-daughter. Thought? Well, God knows, he probably was, in his own little ivy-covered way. I detested the notion. That—excuse my strong language, but I don't mince words—little sharp-tongued, greedy bitch of a step-daughter of mine, I believed, would ruin him if she got hold of him. Fortunately she made the acquaintance of this guitar-playing Hunter person and promptly declared herself in love with him, abandoning her little game of stringing Fred Willis along."

"I thought you didn't care for Lorenzo Hunter," I opined. "He sounds like a prize, especially if he succeeded in putting Dr. Willis back to work at his bunsen burner."

"Personally," answered the board chairman, chest inflating to a noticeable degree, "I find the idea of a grown man making his way along life's rocky road by plucking out little tunes on a guitar an unrealistic, uncourageous, unmasculine means of meeting the challenge of the male sex. But to answer your question, yes, Hunter's alliance with Shirley was fortunate."

A creeping smile lit his face maliciously.

"My duty to my step-daughter consisted of feeding her an endless supply of cash. I felt it my duty out of deference to her departed mother. A sweet woman, although she didn't have any guts. Always crocheting. Never mind. What was I saying?"

"You had been feeding your step-daughter endless supplies of cash," I said wistfully.

"Oh, yes. To be frank, for quite some time I'd been seeking an excuse to cut off his fountainhead of wealth and still appear a normal and dutiful father. Naturally all my friends would understand that I wouldn't want Shirley to marry a shiftless itinerant string-plucker, oh, no!"

He raised his hands in feigned horror. Then he chuckled slyly, as though he had just swallowed three corporations and a holding company. "Heh-heh. I simply cut Shirley off without a cent, before she had time to protest. Wasn't a thing she could do. So off she bounced, presumably to indulge in the free-love activities for which musicians and their ilk are famous. Dr. Willis promptly disappeared. I assumed he was wallowing in sentimentality, off boozing it up, and would be back after a few days. He hasn't returned. It's been over a week."

"Wait a second," I said, leaping up, putting ideas together. "A witness up at Mohawk Mountain saw someone leaving Lorenzo Hunter's cottage around the time of the murder. Maybe you've pegged Dr. Willis all wrong. Could he have driven up there with a rod and blasted Shirley and the man who stole her away from him?"

"That is possible," said Magruder. "That is why the police are looking for him."

"And that crummy Sturns bunch is on his trail, too. If you didn't care for Shirley—were glad to get rid of her, in fact —why bother to put the agency after him? Wasted dough—"

"The hell it's wasted!" erupted F. X. "There's Nirvana!"

"If you're trying to make some sort of point, you're doing a swell job of hiding it."

At that juncture F. X. Magruder cocked his hard blue eye and nailed me down again. "By God, not a man in this company would dare talk to me in that manner. Heh-heh-heh. I must say you don't particularly care whether you lose a commission or not. Or could it be that your smart-aleck remarks are just your means of drawing information out of me?"

Tenting my fingertips together and resuming my seat I sighed, "F. X., you're my kind."

"Look here!" he exclaimed, beating the desk top a couple of times for effect. "Someone is talking of a hundred thousand dollars in connection, apparently, with my step-daughter. And therefore with UPI. That spells one thing. A leak on the Nirvana project. Willis' baby, you understand. At the time he vanished he was putting the last touches on the new drug application we must submit to those bureaucrats at the Food and Drug Administration in Washington. Case histories, evidence of safety—a lot of rot, but it's a sop to respectability. I'm interested in profit margins, Havoc. Nirvana is the best damned thing that's come along in years for nervous old biddies with the flutters and female complaints. And over the years, you see, I've developed a kind of personal rivalry with those bastards in South Bend. They're as unprincipled a bunch of bastards as any on the face of God's earth."

"Which unprincipled bastards are you speaking about?" I inquired.

"The bastards running Rx Corporation. Why, in the past, when UPI has been close to a major break-through on a new drug, they've actually planted spies in our labs and manufacturing sections, just to try and beat us on the market with a similar compound. Believe me, Havoc, it's a law in pharmaceuticals—first on the market means first in sales. They're completely without decency or morals in that firm. Now I'm not above putting in a little mike and tape recorder in their board room—they always rip them out before I get very much, anyway—but trying to shanghai my employees with huge bribes is another thing. Let alone putting paid informers right on my own firing line!"

Drawing a great breath, F. X. Magruder leaped from his chair and flung wide his arms. "Willis may have been kidnapped by the sons of bitches!"

At last a glimmer began to invade my brain. "You mean that Dr. Willis and-or the information about Nirvana which he posssesses might be worth a hundred grand in terms of re-sale to the South Bend crowd?"

"That's what I mean," cried F. X., sinking down in his chair with a dismal sigh.

"Then I've been in the wrong racket all my life. This pill business—"

Magruder shuddered distastefully and covered his eyes. "Please, please. Never call them pills. Never, Havoc. They're pharmaceutical products," he breathed in reverent awe.

"Yes, sir," I replied, bowing my head in shame. "But to resume. Could it be possible that Willis was not lured away at all, but went to them willingly? Maybe he got a little sick of this outfit because of the way Shirley treated him. Love can play a lot of screwy tricks."

"You cannot convince me that Fred Willis sold out," sternly returned the board chairman. "He was a very loyal worker. He had lot of nice stock options, as well as extra participation in our fringe benefit program. Besides, he received his ten-year watch fob only last April. I can tell when a man's loyal and when he isn't."

Magruder stared at me in a most penetrating way, indicating that he had some considerable doubts about my loyalty, too.

"If a bunch of hoodlums got their hands on Willis," I persisted, "could they negotiate with the, ah, South Bend bastards for a hundred thousand dollars or so?"

"They could indeed. Those bastards would sell out their grandmothers. I wish to heaven the Sturns people had put that tape recorder in a better place last time."

Quickly he opened a drawer, took out a memo pad and pencil, scribbled. "By God, I'll just ream them out for it. Next time they'd better do the job right and put it in the executive wash room. I'll probably pick up more information there than in all their damned board meetings combined." Off again, F. X. studied the pads, shaking his head in satisfaction. "Something about the camaraderie of the bathroom that loosens a man's tongue . . ."

"You see?" I exclaimed, breaking in on his scatological monologue. "If the Sturns boys can't even bug a room and keep it bugged, how do you expect them to locate Willis for you? Obviously what you need is someone who can move fast and dig him out, or at least find out whether he's gone over to the rival side. If he has, UPI may be on its fanny as far as being first in the market, but at least the information would help you plan your strategy. You need a representative who can get the job done right away, F. X."

With a slam of a drawer F. X. Magruder put the pad out of sight.

"I have some doubts about your ability to perform that job, Havoc. You may, however, try it, if you wish."

"I wish."

Allowing my natural enthusiasm to get the better of me, I erupted from my chair, perched on the corner of his polished desk, and while F. X. was still befuddled and aghast at this desecration, I pumped his hand in a violent manner.

"And the price we discussed—ten thousand dollars, five in advance for a retain—"

Zip, back went his hand as though I were a member of the unclean.

"Don't be absurd."

"What? Listen, do you think I'm going to tackle a mess like this for nothing?"

"That is entirely up to you, Havoc," he answered, as though reproving one of his junior executives who had bumped him accidentally in the hallway. For a moment I had the sickest of feelings, imagining my sorely-needed commission trickling down an invisible but painfully real drainpipe.

"Ten thousand dollars is quite a fair price," he said.

I practically fell off his desk and lost myself in the wilds of his carpet nap.

"It is?"

"Paid, of course, upon production of some sort of tangible results. Find out whether Willis has . . ." A shudder stirred him. ". . . has sold out to the enemy or has been dealt with in an illegal manner, and you may collect. I told you it would be difficult for me to pry that much money out of the hands of my treasurer Fuddleson. I have no intention of attacking such a gargantuan project merely on the strength of a short interview. As we used to say in my boyhood town of Lumpp's Falls, Ohio, if you think you're going to get five thousand dollars in advance, you are barking up the wrong stump, you dirty dog. Heh-heh-heh."

"So you think I'm going to tackle the whole damned business just on speculation?" I howled.

Thomas F. X. Magruder arose, swelled his chest and fixed his hard blue eye upon me in a most cynical manner.

"Yes, I think you will, Havoc. I am, I believe I may say again with confidence, a sound judge of character. Yours strikes me as shady in the extreme. Your suit is expensively tailored. So, too, are your tastes." Leaning forward with a satanic leer he whispered, "We understand one another, you greedy little wretch."

I complained. "I don't take that kind of abuse from just anyone, you know."

I paused.

I sniffed.

I waited.

"Two hundred dollars in expenses?"

"In advance?" he roared, practically blasting me back out the door.

"Look, you old pirate!" I cried. "My auto doesn't run on tap water! Maybe I'll just trot myself down to South Bend and see whether those bastards are really such bastards after all. Who knows? They might be very generous parties to deal with."

Halting, I sucked a deep breath. Ah, victory. Once more Thomas F. X. Magruder had invaded the confines of one of his desk drawers, taken his pad and was scribbling. He chuckled to himself like a nut as he wrote.

"Downstairs. Heh-heh. I'll make it three hundred. God, you're a regular robber baron. Stop at the cashier's cage. Heh-heh. Fuddleson will be here at five-fifteen with the chit in his hand, howling like he's been castrated. Heh-heh. You're almost as dishonest, in some respect as—well, beside the point. Here."

Into my eager hand he thrust the hastily penned note. Then his roguish manner disappeared.

"Havoc, unless you produce results, the Acme Collection Agency will follow you to the ends of the earth and redeem my three hundred dollars out of your flesh, a cubic inch at a time. Furthermore, I personally promise that if you have bilked me, I'll—"

"Good day, F.X.," said I, before I found out exactly what gruesome thing he would do.

Chapter 4

PERHAPS IT WAS all a fickle financial dream.

Perhaps the references of good old Eddie Sparks and his equally kindly companion Miami Joe Jalasca—both employed by that tower of civic virtue Charles (Candy) Cain—to a hundred thousand smackers and the pill business were a few miles apart from a happy-pill called Nirvana and a nostrum factory called UPI. But of such slender threads are expensive rugs for my flat, as well as nooses of execution, woven.

No good case, assignment or commission rap, call it what you will, had I had for several months. The tellers at my bank didn't quite refuse to honor my checks drawn on *Cash*, not quite yet, but that hour was not long in striking. Thus I leaped to the challenge which the old bandit Magruder had flung.

If I avoided the perils represented by Candy Cain and his boys, I would only have to face the minions of the Acme Collection Agency. It did not seem possible that I could get into trouble with both. Sheer cowardice aside, I even relished the notion of getting in a few licks at Cain. So I dressed nattily when the sun went down that evening and proceeded directly to The French Quarter.

Now if you have ever been foolish enough to press a fevered tenner into the oiled little palm of the headwaiter, getting thereby a bad, small table way up in the fourth tier near the light box, you are acquainted with this large, noisy watering place.

The guests consist mainly of tourists and six daily newspaper columnists who wouldn't go unless they were admitted free. For ten bucks minimum and another ten cover charge you may sink your molars into a thin, stringy steak sandwich while gazing for an hour and a half upon a floorshow featuring unthin and unstringy lovelies in profusion. These broads number twenty-four in the dancing chorus and another dozen, none below six feet five inches, called variously showgirls, models, mannequins or just plain nekkid broads.

Having a certain modest reputation and being a friend of the deceased Lorenzo, I managed to avoid salving the headwaiter's palm and negotiated my way to the bar, where I warmed myself with a Scotch on the rocks and watched the final ten minutes of the stage performance through a glass wall.

The scene on the horseshoe stage represented some sort of Trinidadian village, with all the chorus boys waving their plumes and their straw hats while the nudes descended from overhead seated in large ornate bird-cages, flounces of parrot-colored feathers over their rumps. A tenor was howling into a backstage microphone. I thought the walls would fall down, it was so noisy. Then, during the final verse, some of the fan-boys rolled onstage a small set-piece resembling a makeshift outdoor showerbath. Under this contraption stood one of the showgirls with a white drapery about her middle and nothing at all upon her large, rosy bosoms. With langorous and sensual motions she reached upward, pulled a string and began to writhe among the drips of water pouring out of the iron tub over her head. Then she started drying herself with a scarlet towel, but seemed to be wet only across the buttocks, as she did not rub the towel anywhere else. Her torso swayed in rhythm to the bongo drums, and it was pretty stimulating, that much I'll say. But then the last tropical rainstorm of the production came along, and the dark-haired lovely who had been bathing vanished behind the gyrations of the chorus line. The curtain descended on the sodden pandemonium and dazed, water-logged conventioneers began to file out from the ringside tables, their shoes squeaking horrendously.

I paid for my drink, said so long to the bartender, and made my way backstage.

Since I had been around The French Quarter once or twice, I knew my way, and was not refused admittance to the sacred confines of those in this kind of show biz, if you wish to call it that. Several of the band members greeted me with condolences about the loss of Lorenzo. I inquired where I might find Lorenzo's dressing room. They indicated a chamber at the end of a brick corridor, most all of the musicians then leaving to run out for a coffee and danish at a nearby delicatessen.

I navigated through a crowd of feathered cuties, all of them a foot and a half taller than myself, and arrived at the band room slightly unnerved by the sight of so many ample breasts floating by me at precisely eye level. A lone drummer, changing out of his white show dinner jacket, led me past a makeup table piled with ashtrays, sheet music and racing forms, to a rank of green metal lockers. The drummer, who was wearing a Yale-type striped cap, swept it off his head and pointed.

"Right there, Johnny. Old Lorenzo's locker. Nobody's touched it. Don't know what's in it, either. Lorenzo didn't have any family. Maybe we should get rid of the stuff, but nobody had the heart to do it." The drummer sniffed. "He was a sweet guy, even if he was a hick. You looking for anything in particular?"

"I'm not sure," I responded truthfully. "I'm on an assignment. Just a try."

The drummer replaced his cap, blinking mistily, and journeyed out, stuffing a racing sheet in his pocket on the way.

None of the lockers were protected by padlocks, so I opened Lorenzo's and spent five minutes examining its thin contents.

A white dinner jacket. Black tuxedo trousers. A slightly malodorous boiled shirt. A pair of tasseled loafers. In addition, one half-empty carton of cigarettes. A small black address book shoved back into one corner.

This I thumbed thoroughly, hoping to find a pregnantly significant name. There was not an entry out of the total of close to a hundred that didn't belong to a female. All had such cryptic and licentious notations as, *Likes upon awakening, with smell of coffee perking.* Or, *Will for ten-dollar bottle of perfume but worth it.* Or, *Likes only after eating chop suey or seeing a Western picture.* Lorenzo Hunter, for all his rural nature, had met some fascinating types. Not one offered me any leads as to what I might be looking for, though I did pass an erotic moment dwelling on the notion of making love immediately following a chop suey dinner and/or a Hoot Gibson film.

In that way, I completely missed the entrance of the shower lady.

When I replaced the address book, shut the locker and turned, I yiped. ´

Having come up quiet as a ghost, she now towered over my head, all six feet and at least six inches of her. Further, she hadn't removed the white drapery which hung in a wicked curve just below her navel. Her easily forty-four breasts were scantily concealed by the scarlet towel across her shoulders. A young chick, with gleaming dark hair, she was scented with a perfume so strong I began to feel faint. Leaning down, she smiled at me with large, invitingly red lips.

When I stop to analyze it, the smile was wood all the way through. At the moment, however, as she inched me backward against the locker and bid me welcome with every inch of her quivering and provocative frame, I was too fuddled to do more than paste an inane grin upon my map and grab my porkpie from my head.

"Looking for the showers?" I remarked.

"Looking for you," she said, placing one crimson-nailed hand on my trembling cheek.

Oh, mother. I was outnumbered, outweighed and cheerfully defenseless.

"You're John Havoc, aren't you? Lorenzo's friend? I remember you were here the night the boys in the band gave him an engagement party after the last show. Poor Lorenzo. He was so gentle, so nice."

Trying to relegate the beating of my ductless glands to a role of lesser importance, I noticed she had delivered the last lines with a hollow sincerity. She had a dumb, somewhat nasal manner of talking. Not that I would have minded, ordinarily. Only it seemed that she had introduced ·the subject of Lorenzo Hunter in a rather forced way. I wondered why.

"Mr. Havoc," she purred, toying with the scarlet towel in a revealing manner, "would you like to come up to my place after we close down tonight?"

"Thanks, doll. Love to. But I don't even know your name. I insist on formality."

"Not too much formality, I hope," she cooed, back in a familiar element. She was listening to me, but her hips were still hearing bongo drums. Oh, those tropical love-feasts. I received a massage from the upper portion of her anatomy. "Not too much?" she cooed again.

"The name," I said, sidling along the lockers. "Then we can discuss—"

"Rosalind del Rio. I take a shower every night on stage, just like this."

"I know, I know," I croaked in feeble tones. "No need to demonstrate."

Something in her approach, inviting though it was, put little alarm clocks ringing in my headbox. I had indeed been introduced to her at the backstage engagement party for Lorenzo, but had been given the prompt freeze an undersized gentleman deserves. On that occasion I had not been worth bothering about. Now I was receiving an invitation to her bower of love, if that's what you want to call it.

I determined to meet fire with ice.

"Lady, I don't know exactly what you're fishing for. In the first place, any doll named Rosalind del Rio is strictly phony. You can start by being a little more frank—and I don't mean that way," I added with a strangled cry, as she manipulated the scarlet towel and her breasts peeped in and out of view in a manner she doubtless thought fetching. I poked a butt between my lips and stiffened to my full height.

"If you're trying to suck something out of me, talk plain or beat it."

"Why, dear little Johnny, that's a terrible crude way to talk. I just happened to catch sight of you out in the hallway. I thought, what a perfect chance to ask you a question and get acquainted, too."

One of her hands, experimenting with the white drapery around her moving hips, helped clarify exactly how she wished to get acquainted. She drew her lips out in a luscious but hundred percent ersatz pout.

"I'm disappointed that you're treating me like this. Why, I remember at Lorenzo's party, I thought you were absolutely exotic—so wiry and virile-looking." Practically submerging me under her lips and her perfume, she added in a provocative way, "I thought having a lover like you would be so original."

"You didn't think it at the party," I commented sourly, ducking out from under her descending mammaries. "If my memory serves, I might as well have been manufactured of Pittsburgh Plate Glass. Look, Miss del Rio, let's quit bulling, huh? Tell me what you want."

"Didn't I tell you what I wanted, lover?" she sighed, massaging her creamy thighs.

"Horse offal, if you will pardon my saying so. I don't believe a word of this act you're giving me, starting with the name bit and ending with your sudden desire to get me on your mattress. As I stated a few minutes ago, clarify things or shut the hell up. All right?"

For a moment dumb-broad consternation possessed her. Half a dozen expressions chased each other across her painted face. I waited, puffing my smoke, until she chose the one which she thought would win me over. It happened to be a simpering palsy-walsy grin which was intended, I suppose, to suggest that Our Bare Essences were exposed and all was frankly shown at last. This smirking continued for a moment. I turned away disgustedly.

"Wait, Johnny! Don't leave! I'm so sorry. You're perfectly right. If you're going to be honest with me, I have to be the same. Nakedly honest." A wiggle, a bump.

"So I'm waiting. You can speak your piece until I get bored."

A flicker in her darkish eyes told me I had angered her. Furthermore, that in other circumstances she would have belted me, or perhaps picked me up and tried to slap me across her knee. The sweet and tender understanding on her

face, however, altered only slightly. In a conspiratorial manner she whispered, "Let's start off fresh and clean. I'm not
honestly Rosalind del Rio. The real me is Rose-Edna Klutz,
and I was born in Gas City, Indiana."

"Figures," I remarked, dusting a fallen ash from the toe
of my loafers.

"You say the cutest things, Johnny! You're a sweet, absolutely sweet little man."

"Then quit calling me a son of a bitch with your cute,
sweet dark eyes, Rose-Edna."

That cracked her nicely. She advanced several steps, her
platform heels clacking in a menacing way. Her long-nailed
hands drew in, cat-wise.

"Damn you, you wise little jerk!" she snarled. "I try to
be nice to you, and what do I get? Lousy insults! All right,
damn it, I tried. We'll play it on your terms. Honest and
nasty. About Lorenzo Hunter—"

"The name is not familiar," I said, grinning in irritating
fashion.

"No? It better be, you sawed-off jerk. I want to know
what became of Lorenzo's property."

"What property, Rose-Edna Klutz?"

When I said that, I thought she would slug me. I retreated
a judicious pair of paces. "Besides, what difference should it
make to you what became of Lorenzo's mysterious property,
as you call it? If I knew anything about what you're babbling
over, I wouldn't tell you anyway. Not unless your name isn't
honest-to-gosh Klutz, but you're Shirley Magruder in disguise.
I doubt it."

Tipping my porkpie, I prepared to depart from the dressing chamber, hearing a stir in the corridor outside that informed me a few of the band members were returning. I had
taken but half the steps required to exit myself from the
room when Rosalind's claws damaged my suit, chewed my
shoulder and caused me to whirl around in an excess of
temper. Before I could clout her, she yelled:

"Listen to me, worm! You know damned well what I'm
talking about. There were some valuable documents—if
you've laid your greasy little paws on them—"

"Documents?" I spoke blandly. "Like Lorenzo's musician's union card, you mean?"

"Damned little bastard!" she howled, driven past all subtlety.

Away fell the scarlet towel as she took a poke. I nailed her wrist in my right hand, held it static for a minute even though her writhings almost lifted me clean off the concrete floor, then pushed her not-so-gently away from me. Lunging, she flailed her arms wildly, skidded and snatched up the towel. When I turned to see what had caused her sudden pause in battle, I noticed that a group of the band boys had assembled in the doorway, leering. The drummer clapped appreciatively for the entertainment we had been providing. I bowed low, retrieved my fallen lid and turned my back on Rosalind del Rio, determined to vacate the vicinity before she got a half-nelson on me. Several of the bandsmen expressed regret that I had not pasted Rosalind del Rio in the snout, declaring her a regular bitch with which to work.

"Sorry, gang," I answered in jolly tones. "She's a lady, somewhere underneath that crude exterior. Although I must say they do raise 'em wild in Gas City."

"Don't let that little creep get away!" came an outraged shriek as I darted into the hall.

I commenced a swift route of travel out the stage-side exit into the club area, and thence to the bar, wishing to put additional distance between myself and the naked harridan. It had been, I reflected, a zany interlude, with many half-hidden elements whose significance I did not fully grasp. On the other hand, as I proceeded to the horseshoe bar, it came to me that perhaps beneath the coo-coo dialogue ran a real streak of danger. I could have played it all wrong. A nasty suspicion was ripening in my dome, one which would bear checking with a favorite source of information.

Rosalind's performance had been so badly played—she was such an obviously dumb, stacked chick—that I would have made myself ludicrous trying to talk things over. Yet certain other modes of behavior, which I might call ludicrous, too, could spell out that old debbil Trouble. I sensed a connection.

Yes, must check, Mr. Havoc. Soon. You may have concocted a worse little jam..

I began to wonder about the documents she'd mentioned. Documents? What docu—

"Mr. Havoc? Hey, hang on . . ."

I swiveled my skull absently, saw the bartender pointing to a shadowy corner of his premises.

"Gentleman down there asking for friends of Lorenzo Hunter. I didn't know whether you'd be back this way. He seems pretty anxious."

"They're thick as fleas tonight, aren't they? Here."

Leaving a bill in the bartender's startled mitts, I navigated around the mahogany curve of the bar. It had only two customers at this between-shows hour, an elderly Sioux City matron at one end drinking a Tom Collins and reading a guide book, and an elusive, inquisitive shadow at the other. Another of Lorenzo's friends, non-existent when he was up on the band stand twanking his guitar, aswarm on the landscape and buzzing with consideration now that he had expired. I leered and peered, trying to make out the nature of the seated shadow.

"Were you looking for me, friend? My name is John Havoc. The bartender said—"

"I'm looking for you if you knew Lorenzo Hunter very well. Did you?"

"Lots of people seem to think so. Cost you a fast drink if you want to make a pitch."

The shadow growled, "I wanted to talk about a hundred thousand dollars. And Nirvana."

"Put your cash back, stranger. I'll buy the round."

Chapter 5

As CHRIS THE bartender deposited a pair of Scotches over ice, my more or less spiritual companion slid a square of white pasteboard along the polished wood. Finely and discreetly embossed thereon was the name *Gray B. Ainslee.* Below that, *Manufacturer's Representative.*

I slid it back to him. He solidified a little, bending forward into the pale blue light of the bulbs on the backbar. Gray B. Ainslee, hunched upon his stool in a Rodinish posture, looked as though he might be taller than Rosalind del Rio when unwound. In addition, his thick shoulders filled an expensive dark suit like bars of pig lead with muscular bumps on them. He had a reddish face, a hawk nose, thinning blond hair and a soft accent that might have been touched with Baltimorian or D.C.-ese. To make matters worse, he appeared to like to smile all the time, as though he swallowed his lesser unfortunates for breakfast.

"Your card confuses me, Gray B.," I remarked. "I'm not set up to distribute any of your goods, whatever the line. I don't distribute anything but money. And that only when I have some. And then only to waiters, taxi-cab drivers and ladies of ill repute."

"Doggone," Gray B. Ainslee laughed, like a defrosting icebox. "You got a sense of humor."

"Debatable. But I've bought you a drink. I expect a return on the money."

With furtive glances to right and left he asked, "This a safe place to talk?"

"Unless that old bag with the travel folder is an operative of the Federal Trade Commission, I imagine it's as good as any. You turned pale just then, Gray B."

"I don't want dealings with the damned government in any way, shape or form."

With a jerk he upended his Scotch on the rocks and swallowed it whole, letting some of the icecubes go flying in his careless haste. Closing both his hands around the glass and setting it with a firm clank upon the wood, he said:

"Just tell me one thing, Mr. Havoc. How close were you to Lorenzo Hunter? Close enough to know what I'm talking about when I say Nirvana?"

"Closer, coz." I gave him a confidential nudge. "You working for South Bend?"

"That may be true," he drawled. "On the other hand, I'm

not opening my lip too dang far, you can be sure of it.
Lorenzo was arranging to get his hands on a certain article
for which my client—anonymous, you understand—was willing to pay one hundred thousand dollars, including ten percent commission for my part in securing it. Now Lorenzo
Hunter is dead. I didn't know him well. I haven't got access
to his personal effects. Even so, I damn sure have a few connections around town. Enough to buy some information from
the local police. It so happens the article I mentioned was
not among his effects."

"That article being," I said in my most slyly oracular style,
"a document?"

Gray B. Ainslee's eyes went down to mere slits.

"I guess you're a pretty good friend. You wouldn't even
know what I was talking about if you weren't."

"I've told you my half of it, brother. From now on, any
deal you want from me, you'll have to work for. Let's just get
another round of drinks, for which you'll pay this time, naturally, and use the interlude to chat about this document."

As I gabbled, my dome kept grinding, scheming, planning,
until at last I thought I had maneuvered things to exactly
where I wanted them.

"Tell me all about it, Gray B."

"You have quite a bit of crust, I must admit that," replied
the representative.

I laid my hand on his shoulder.

"Want to call it an evening? Inform your clients that the
document has disappeared, sorry, but they can save their
hundred grand? You'll just skip the tidy little commission,
too. What's ten thousand?"

Gray B. Ainslee scowled at me. This I ignored, bulling my
way forward: "No, Gray B., I have already spent a few
rounds tonight discussing matters by the oblique. I'm tired of
it. You know I'm a friend of Lorenzo Hunter's. If we're to
conduct any business, I want a full and complete account of
your position. Client and all. Or nothing doing."

He blinked. "I got half a notion to smack you in the
mouth."

"But the other and smarter half tells you that you better not, unless you don't need the ten grand. Now cease the unfriendly gestures. Unburden your soul. Spill it quickly, in a couple or three sentences, and you'll find yourself wondrously healed and relieved."

"Are you a nut or something?" he inquired. "You sure you knew Lorenzo?"

"The document," I harangued. "The document, the document."

Sighing in defeat, Gray B. seized his glass once more and jolted its entire contents into his innards, allowing a horrible shudder to activate his shoulder blades.

"Damn it, you got me over the barrel, Havoc. My Hotsy Totsy Barbecue Briquette line is going to the dogs. Nobody wants to move carloads of turkey plumes the way money's so tight these days. Tiger Thompson just dropped dead of a coronary last week and I'm paying storage on a warehouse full of autographed jock straps won't sell worth a crap now that old Tiger's dead. Christ, business is awful. I need that money."

I thought it impossible for his lamps to grow more slitted, but they did. In a threatening way he growled, "I guess we have to do business. But you know right enough what I'm after. The photostat copy of the FDA application form UPI on Nirvana. Formula. Manufacturing processes. Clinical study reports. The works. A big book this thick."

He showed me how thick. "I want it. You get it. I can arrange to scrounge four percent off the client, exclusive of my commission—"

"Give me your client's name, Gray B.," I whispered insinuatingly.

"I'm taking my neck in my hands telling you as much as I have already!"

Executing a shrug, I remarked, "I can't think of a soul who'd want a Tiger Thompson jock strap any more. Or a box of turkey plumes. Or even some Hotsy Totsy Barbecue Briquettes. It seems to me the only good goods you're pushing is the application copy."

With a huff and a sigh Gray B. summoned the bartender, ordered another Scotch, and when that had been poured down his maw, he said desperately, "All right, all right, you

little needling gangster. But you better get results once I
spill the deal. Of course it's Rx Corporation, South Bend.
Who the hell else could it possibly be? Now I want the
document. And I want it mighty fast, see? Unless I can deliver before many more days pass, that South Bend crew is
going to thumb its nose at me and call in another middle-
man."

"Hang on, Gray B.," I remarked, climbing from my stool,
thoughts a-whizzing. "I can get an answer one way or
another after one quick phone call."

"Phone call!" he exclaimed apoplectically, upsetting the
remains of his drink. "If you're going to try and blow the
whistle on me, I'll wring your neck right now."

But before the luckless turkey-plume vendor could clamp
hands on my windpipe, I had darted around the bar, tip-
toed through the litter of bus tour travel brochures surrounding the Collins-swacked matron, and sought sanctuary
in the last stuffy booth of three in the foyer's telephone
corner.

As I argued with the night switchboard girl out at the
UPI plant, I caught sight of Gray B. making sure I would not
escape him. He stationed himself half a dozen feet from the
booth, puffing on a smoke. He squinted from his nervous
salesman's red face and munched from time to time on a
hangnail.

Eventually I wormed Thomas F. X. Magruder's home
telephone number from the plant girl. After this I was sub-
jected to considerable abuse by the board chairman himself,
who had been cozily curled up in the rack with a spicy novel.
Managing to make my point finally clear, I shouted, purred,
blustered and wheedled for ten minutes. I emerged at last
from the booth with a strangled cry for air, a damp forehead and a certain feeling of satisfaction.

I hissed at Gray B. Ainslee. He joined me promptly. He
had a height edge of a foot and a half, and I found myself
mystically fascinated by the neurotic jumps of his Adam's
apple as he gulped, swallowed and sucked nicotine smoke
while I told him:

"Relax, old friend. Everything is arranged. I've been talking with my client—"

"Client?" he howled. "Client? You never said you had a client, you little—"

"A little louder, Gray B.," I invited. "Perhaps the management will put you on stage for the next show and let you tell it to all the conventioneers. What makes you think you have any monopoly on working for another party, pill companies included?"

One might have thought he had been observing the internal revenue investigator examine his tax return. He gargled and gurgled in horror.

"Pill . . . did you . . . did you say pill?"

"I said pill, indeed. Concretely, I mean Pharmaceuticals, Incorporated."

"Oh, you conniving, sawed-off son of a bitch!" he howled again, much to the consternation of the headwaiter lounging nearby.

With lowered shoulders and bunched fists, Gray B. Ainslee laid decorum aside and prepared to lay me right next to it with a couple of clouts in the puss. I danced and parried, causing a highly unusual scene in the night club foyer. The headwaiter, wringing his dollar-caressed palms, angled toward us.

"Gentlemen, gentlemen, we simply can't have a scene of this kind going on in—"

I managed to maneuver the headwaiter between me and my antagonist. The latter trumpeted wrathfully, "Get out of the way, greasy! I'm going to tear off the little rat's limbs and tie them around his neck in a ribbon. Damn you, I said get out of my way!"

Klop. The unfortunate headwaiter receved a cut in the chops which disarranged his hairpiece sideways upon his dome. As he reeled, this indignity became apparent. With shrieks of a wounded ego plaintively upon his lips, he struggled to right his rug.

Gray B. Ainslee let go a haymaker. I bent over as if to tie a shoelace. He exclaimed in excruciating pain as his knuckles conked the wall. At this juncture several specimens considerably more athletic than the unmanned headwaiter were covering from the area of the club proper. Applying a wrenching grip to Gray B. Ainslee's flailing right arm, I exclaimed softly, "Let's get out of here, friend. Together or separately. If you would rather make ten grand instead of twenty . . ."

"Twenty? Is this a gag? Little buddy, it better not be a gag or I'll personally take you—"

"Quit babbling before the goon squad collars us."

I half-threw him down the red plush of the club's front stairs. I whistled and made Indian signs to the busty maid behind the hat check stand.

"Peaches, the lid, quick!"

She scaled my porkpie across the foyer like it was an outer-space vehicle. I nabbed it on the fly and ran. When we neared the street level, the crowd of four burlies was eight steps behind us, cursing in an ungentlemanly way and urging us to wait so they could pound hell out of us. In their midst, as I held glass street doors open for the slightly confused Gray B., I spied the poor headwaiter urging his toadies on to faster pursuit, a flap of his toupee dangling uncemented over his right eye. I gave Gray B. a slight kick in the rump to urge him along. I seized the seams of his suitcoat shoulders and hurled him to the left.

"The automat around the corner! Quick! There's no extradition treaty. We ought to be able to dodge them. Come on, Gray B., shake it!"

Thus we arrived at the Orn & Ardmore Vend-O-Treat Automatic Cafeteria. I crashed our way through the line in a most unceremonious fashion, Gray B. ending up with a dish of chocolate pudding and I with a revolting kidney-bean salad. I flung money at the cashier lady, noting on the sidewalk the four heavies in tuxedos glowering in a most unfriendly fashion through the window panes. I yanked Gray B.'s sleeve.

"This way. We'll throw ourselves on the mercy of the law."

Baffled, he stumbled after me to a table where a lone member of the city's finest was taking a moment out to refresh himself with a chicken pot pie, a plate of spaghetti and a milkshake.

"Mind if we join you, officer?" I questioned, smiling. "Seems crowded in here." I waved at several dozen empty tables. "Thanks a lot, officer. I'd like you to meet my friend Clyde Bungsdorf. Clyde, shake hands with one of the guardians of law and order, making our streets safe for democracy."

I forced Gray B.'s hand into the spaghetti-stained paw of the baffled cop, who was scowling and preparing to unloose his billy and clout us for drunks. In a secretive manner I glanced to the window. I saw the four bouncers retreating into the darkness in a pet of frustration. Swooping up my kidney-bean salad I exclaimed, "Come on, Gray B., I don't think we're welcome here. Let's find another table, back there in the corner."

Settled at last, I gave my kidney salad to Gray B. who shoved it into his mouth in alternate bites with the chocolate pudding. The bemused officer wandered to the cashier and pointed to us, but the lady shook her head, offering him no help. Finally the minion left the establishment, lingering on the sidewalk several moments to survey me suspiciously. I breathed in somewhat easier fashion, ignored the bull and concentrated on Ainslee. He was just polishing off the last of the pudding with large smacking sounds. Apparently the excitement of our little adventure had upset his emotional balance and made necessary an immediate offering to his aroused gastric juices.

"Oh, my God, my ulcer," he moaned piteously.

"I don't give a hoot about your ulcer. You nearly landed both of us in jail with your headstrong behavior. Didn't I mention something about twenty thousand dollars?" I barked.

"You did," Gray B. replied, clutching his midsection in an anguished way. "That's . . . *ugh* . . . that's . . . oh, God, my soda pills . . ."

Taking a bottle of these from his pocket, he ingested half a dozen and mumbled through the mouthful. ". . . that's . . . *urp* . . . all that keeps me from . . . *urgch* . . . knocking your conniving little . . . *arg* . . . head off right now. You told me you were working for UPI and that's enough to make me rip

you in eighteen pieces . . . because . . . *arg, arg!* . . . I've
been working against you right from the beginning."

"Too true," I answered. "Howsoever, while I do not have
the document which you are seeking for your client, I think
I can get it." That was sheer braggodocio, but Gray B. had
no idea. "And rather soon, too. That's why I telephoned my
personal friend and employer, Tom Magruder. Good old F.X.
Board chairman of UPI, you know. Good old guy."

Ainslee scowled and belched an additional time.

"Keep talking. It's safer for you," he said.

I executed a sly shrug. "Here's the scheme. When I recover the copy of the application you stand to make exactly
double the ten percent commission promised by the South
Bend mob. Namely twenty thousand clams. All you have to
do," I whispered, "is make sure that a copy of the Nirvana
application is delivered to your client on schedule."

Gray B. appeared ready to fall off his chair.

"You need a head-shrinker, little buddy."

"Not necessarily, pal. Consider the intricacies of the pharmaceutical jungle. That wily old crook Magruder stood to
lose a fat market advantage if your client got hold of the
application. But now, when I redeem it, UPI does not merely
have to leave the situation static, but can repay Rx for its
dastardly maneuvering. Oh, the photostat of the application
you'll deliver will look authentic enough. I can't give you
too many of the details—Magruder's lab laddies will have
to work them out. I just handed him the suggestion and he
bit all the way. He's as larcenous as either one of us. Point is,
Gray B., the copy you deliver to your clients will be a three-
dollar bill from the start."

I chuckled insidiously. "When the South Bend crew tries
to manufacture Nirvana according to the processes outlined
in that little old document, they'll gum up all their ma-
chinery so badly they won't produce a pill till next St. Swith-
in's day. Magruder is absolutely sure his brains can fix it up
to look authentic. And totally phony."

A most predatory leer lighted the countenance of the
manufacturer's representative.

"That old fraud Magruder is prepared to . . . ah . . . pay twenty thousand if I deliver it?"

"That is the figure he quoted, yes. Since he will owe me a considerable sum also when the job is completed, I will personally guarantee that both of us will receive our just reward. Or I'll topple his little old house of cards for fair. What do you say? What can you possibly lose?"

"More commissions from Rx, for one thing," meditated my companion greedily.

In an absent manner I regarded the flourescent ceiling fixtures of the automatic cafeteria.

"That's an item you must square with your conscience, good old Gray B. Whether you wish to keep playing for peanuts the rest of your days or not. Magruder is obviously a much better contact. Out-generalling the South Bend boobs all along the line. But if you're frightened, no guts . . . ah, well. Perhaps I can locate another courageous soul who will—"

My arm was practically wrenched from its socket as Gray B. Ainslee crushed my hand in his salesman's grip.

"Deal, by God! Absolutely, by God! Never let it be said that old Gray Ainslee looked a big deal in the face and was too lily-livered to give it a try . . . *ulch!*"

He seized his stomach area again and rocked back and forth on his chair in the extremes of gastric distress. But he managed to summon a toothsome smile of friendship at the same time.

From my pocket I took a card and pencil and slid them over.

"Scribble down your phone number and stand by. When I get hold of the application, Magruder will want the dummy in South Bend post haste. Be sure I can reach you any time I need you."

"Mind telling me where the application is, old buddy?" commented the representative, scrawling what I had bidden, vestiges of larceny in the sneaky corners of his eyes.

"I can locate it, Gray B. Until I do I'll keep a pat hand."

"Suit yourself. Pleasure doing business with you, little partner."

He rose, uttering a last burbling stomach noise, and flung out his hand again. All the old precepts of the salesman's manual rose in his head.

"Put her there. I like a man with courage and daring. A man who isn't afraid to see the big picture. Right after I get back from South Bend I want to buy you a drink. I've got a little plan cooking for those Tiger Thompson athletic supporters. I think you're the kind of man I need. With a little restitching, we could get rid of that Thompson's autograph on the fly, maybe find some other cheap pug and put his name there instead. Then we airbrush the packages, change Thompson's face and unload 'em. I think you'd be a whiz-bang on the road, little partner. Ever consider going on the road? Plenty of chances for a man to make a killing, and I like a man who isn't afraid."

That was the point at which I abandoned him, on the concrete before the Orn & Ardmore Ven-O-Treat Automatic Cafeteria.

Gray B. Ainslee kept waving and blathering about going on the road and capturing luck by the short hairs, etc. etc. etc., until I had reached the corner and passed under the suspicious and scrutinizing eye of the policeman we'd sat with.

Tipping my porkpie I remarked, "Hope you enjoyed the chicken pot pie, officer."

Before he could arrest me, I leaped into the neon noise of Sidney Sheba's Penny Fun Land, made my way past the girlie viewers and the artillery practice range, and thence to the alley and a parking lot where I had stashed my convertible. I felt fairly high.

But driving through the spring evening scented with exhaust fumes, I suddenly lost all pretensions. So the idea I'd pitched to Magruder had been a good one. One at which the old rat had leaped with unholy relish. So I had convinced Gray B. Ainslee that it would be more profitable to foist off a phony application.

So where in ding-dong hell was I going to turn up the original?

Chapter 6

To ALLOW MYSELF moments to ruminate upon that crucial question, and also to inquire into a connection which had bothered me a few hours earlier, I tooled my convertible into another lot a few blocks away, straightened my necktie and strolled the pavements along to Twenty-Two.

Twenty-Two is that posh establisment with ninety percent of its clientele made up of souls who wish to be listed in the columns as having had the bucks to dine or booze there, plus ten percent composed of oddly assorted night creatures, hustlers and fast buck artists, present company not excluded, who find it a convenient clearing house for all types of low gossip, scurrilous tips and other information not fit to print.

At any given hour, either on the plush upper floors or the checker-clothed rathskeller downstairs, one may sit back and view a noted and grizzled author just up from the Caribbean, his sport shirt open to expose his manly chest hairs, quaffing cocktails with the diva who threw a dish of cole slaw at the manager of a Texas opera company.

These two seated near several professional comedians, one large and fat, one small, one bald with glasses, one with slightly buck teeth, all sharing a table and exchanging jollies, the one telling the most jollies the loudest being the one with the better ratings that week.

These several seated in heady proximity to an ebon-haired Coast lovely, winner of three Academy Awards and breaker of six marriages at the sweet age of only eighteen, conversing with a debonair Latin gentleman, silver-haired and sophisticated, released from Leavenworth two years previous and due to be deported to Sicily next week.

It's a pretty intoxicating zoo if you can afford twenty dollars for a pepper steak, the least expensive item on the French menu. That menu is merely one more gambit to

49

further confuse the hapless tourist who squeaks inside after he tips the doorman lavishly, panting so hard he dislocates his wife's arm and puts a mist on his Kiwanis button.

Over this discreet clip house presides a middle-sized, patrician looking fellow of uncertain years, black-haired, pale-skinned and perpetually disdainful.

"Good evening, Anton," I remarked on entering.

He held out his hand in reflex action. I shook it. This caused his upper lip to writhe automatically. I asked him, "How's about downstairs?"

"I am very sorry, Mr. Havoc," he replied in bad Bela Lugosi dialect. "We're completely booked."

"Why, Anton, unless my old eyes fail, you're none other than Sven Rasmussen, a black Dane whose dear old daddy dirt-farmed in Frozen Falls, Minnesota, where I was born."

"If you promise not to reveal that fact," Sven replied with a wooden map, "I will do what I can to locate a place for you to sit." As he led me belowstairs into the rathskeller with its dozens of model airplanes descending from the ceiling, he whispered from the side of his mouth, "Anything cooking, kid? You've been in absentia a few nights."

"Could be," I mouthed. "Let me get a bite and a jolt and then drop around. Question—"

"Oh, dear, Madame Helga!" cried he, rushing from my side to a minked dowager fussing near the powder room. "So sorry we couldn't seat you immediately! So many people here tonight. Anton's head is simply spinning. But in a moment or two, I promise. Meantime, my dear darling, tell me all the latest! How was the jet trip from Biarritz?"

Passing out of earshot of his professional performance, I seated myself at one of the checkered tables, greeted the waiter Heine, and made a loud show of ordering items from the menu totalling ninety-six dollars nad twelve cents. In five minutes Heine returned bearing three sandwiches of edam cheese on rye and a pilsener glass of beer. I munched and ogled the celebrities until Sven returned and hovered near at hand.

"Now, John, let the freaks shift for themselves a moment. You mentioned a question."

"Could you spare a minute on the telephone if you can't answer me yourself? It's not wildly pressing, but it's bothering me. Would help me know where I'm going."

"You don't know?" he answered with arch mockery. "Ah, civilization collapses."

"Well, I know I'm heading for a pile of green, but I want to find the smoothest route."

"What's the query? Perhaps if I can't supply the answer, one of the staff—"

"I would like to know whether there's any word on a tall bimbo named Rosalind del Rio. She takes a shower bath on stage at the French Quarter every night. Does she have any friends of note? If so, their names and business connections would also be appreciated."

"The French Quarter?" Sven-Anton gasped, nostrils a-quiver. "That gaudy bagino? That temple of godless and noisy philistinism? Um. Perhaps I could have someone telephone Fritz the headwaiter. We don't speak in public, but I play gin with him on Tuesdays."

"That would be appreciated, friend. Kindly don't mention my name. I dropped in there earlier tonight and left under somewhat of a cloud. The posse may still be out."

"I'll do what I can," he replied, winking.

Then he raised his tones and declared for all to hear, "I'm very sorry, sir, that card upon the table expressly states there is a twenty-dollar minimum service charge. If you can't afford Twenty-Two, don't come here."

And off he paraded, leaving me to munch and ruminate further. When he returned ten minutes later the message was short and unwelcome:

"You had better not put in an appearance at The Quarter for a few days, John lad. Apparently you terrorized quite a number of the customers by engaging in a fist fight at the bar. Fritz asked of your whereabouts. Naturally I said nothing, but he's displeased. You may be displeased by the information he offered in regard to your question. The bimbo you described, Miss del Rio, has some unsavory connections. She's currently sharing a bed with a most unwholesome member of the underworld, one whose name I dislike mentioning in such refined surroundings."

Now the nasty connection was firming up for fair.

"Does he eat peppermints?"

"He does, he does. Have you chanced across him? If so, beware."

"I have," I replied in saddened tones. "And I expect I will again before this is over. Thank you, Sven. Just let me sit here and enjoy my despondency."

"Mr. Charles Cain is not the sort one would wish to deal with voluntarily. I have heard it said his temper is uncontrollable. He will stoop to any means to attain an end."

"A few of his cronies have already stooped, as well as stepped. On me."

Casting regretful gazes in my direction, Sven would have continued his advice except for the shrill outcries of Madame Helga in the foyer. Heads turned. Sven became Anton, rushing off to try and salve her fury, doubtless seating her in the powder room, for she never turned up in the rathskeller, at least not for the next ten minutes.

Munching the last of my sandwiches and summoning Heine to settle the bill, I saw Dolores, a charming redhead who runs around the joint snapping suckers' photographs with a Speed Graphic, rushing headlong for my table. Anxiously she waved Heine off. She came up and leaned close, bathing me in perfume and the intoxicating proximity of bosoms popping half out of the top of a stage maid's briefs. I was about to say something idiotic when I noticed a peculiar, intent shine in her dark eyes.

Scared silly . . .

"Johnny," she trembled with a forced smile, "I have those photographs you ordered last week back in the darkroom. Wouldn't you like to come and take a look at them?"

"Photographs?" I questioned. "Dolores, this is J. Havoc, local resident. You've got me mixed up with one of the Dubuque sugar daddies who get in here on off nights."

"Please, please, Johnny!" she said, clutching my arm. "You know the photographs I mean. The ones you were so interested in seeing. You told me you wanted them right away, as soon as they were finished. You haven't come in since then."

Desperately she paused and waved at a drunken customer who kept motioning to have his flick took. "I'll be right there, sir!" I wondered whether she would break into tears this minute or next. "It'll only take a minute, Johnny," she pleaded "It's very important that you come back to the darkroom and look at your pictures."

I stood up, threw away my napkin and said, "Lead the way, Dolores." It's not that I'm stupid. It's just that who wouldn't trust a good kid with bosoms like those?

Like a flushed bird, she practically whizzed through the tables, dragging my hands. Her own flesh felt icy cold. In her pretty little face I'd seen a raw mixture of regret, as though she could hardly bring herself to invite me back to the non-existent darkroom, and pure unvarnished fright.

Dolores opened a gargoyle-carved door and plunged forward. Once we were through the portal into a black hall that smelled of a kitchen nearby, she sobbed. "Oh, Johnny, I'm sorry. I didn't have any choice."

"Choice about what?" I asked brightly, simultaneously catching sight of a large and unpleasant heater gleaming like the very hell in a pool of light at hall's end.

The choice she did not have came instantly clear.

Twenty-Two employed a pair of lady photographers, the other being named Babette. Poor Babette was now standing helplessly under the tin-shaded light, menaced by the afore-mentioned rod as well as another, ogled pitilessly by the owners of these same armaments of destruction. One of the owners bent his lanky frame and emerged from shadows to greet me with a snaggle-tooth grin boding nothing but mayhem.

"Why, hello, midget," was the greeting from the lips of Edward Sparks.

A hand-painted view of the Floridas resting obliquely over a paunch floated into view as Babette and Dolores collapsed against one another, sobbing like a couple of banshees. The owner of the illustrated travel scene menaced me with his weapon in an unlovely manner.

"Lucky you listened to the little dolly, Havoc, because I

told her I'd put some holes in her girl friend if she didn't bring you back with her, and right away."

"Let them go, Jalasca," I said, surprised at my own hard-sounding voice.

"No, let's us go instead, midget," snarled the short-tempered Sparks. "Right out the rear door and into the sedan. Mr. Charlie Cain requests your presence at a little chinfest. Whether it's a round trip is entirely up to you."

He conked me on the head with his heater.

"Hope that's clear, midget man. Shall we proceed?"

Chapter 7

WE ARRIVED AT our destination just as the hands on my wrist clock showed two in the cold, depressing morning.

Tormented by the assorted jabs and pokes delivered to me by Jalasca and Sparks during the ride, my spirits had dropped to a disgustingly low point by the time Sparks pulled the heap to a halt before a residence. It was a brownstone, moldy-looking but situated in a district whose expanded rental scale could hardly be afforded by a medium-time hoodlum unless his ego and his very scratching for existence, or both, demanded maintenance of a reasonably fancy address. But with Jalasca and Sparks gigging me in the short ribs, I hardly gave a good damn whether the place looked like Buckingham Palace. What awaited me had to be dismal.

Exactly how dismal I did not realize until I had been ushered into the great man's presence on the first floor. I found him reclining in a vast red leather chair, slippered feet on a hassock, a quart bottle of beer and a sack of peppermints on a lamp table beside him, and Miss Rose-Edna Klutz standing behind, eyeing me in the manner of a tabby-cat whose fur has recently been kinked in the wrong direction.

Jalasca and Sparks slid closed a pair of wooden doors to my rear. They wandered to a small bar and helped themselves to jolts of high-proof liquor, hardly able to conceal their smug pleasure. Behind the leather job the shower girl reached down to comfortably massage the tired neck muscles of her master. The upper half of what she wore appeared to be a thin butterfly silk robe, bound around the middle with a tassel cord, but hanging open immodestly from that point upward.

Charlie Cain, a fortyish sort, carried a widening paunch beneath his monogrammed shirt. He wore suspenders and herringbone trousers, had wooly graying hair, a flat forehead and thick lips. His hands reminded me of tender cuts of country hams. One of the cuts kept up a continuous movement between his chewing, scrunching mouth and the bag of peppermints.

"A pleasure to meet you, Havoc," he remarked, biting down on a mint with a loud crack.

"Do you mind if I sit down? Or is all the blood supposed to rush out of my head and leave me faint and at your mercy?" I tried to concentrate on him, avoiding Rose-Edna's wrath.

"Very amusing," he said with a frown, as though he was not quite sure what amusing meant. "Eddie boy, get Mr. Havoc that chair over there. See he's nice and comfortable."

As I turned about in natural curiosity, Sparks rushed the arm chair forward over the polished oak floor, rammed its seat against the backs of my knees, and I took an unceremonious tumble.

"Oh, my God!" cried Candy Cain. "Oh, that's rich, that really is."

"You're getting an awful big bang out of the little crudhead, Candy," exclaimed Rose-Edna, withdrawing the ministrations of her hands. "Didn't I tell you how he talked to me at The Quarter? Nasty. Rude. I thought you took care of men who got nasty and—"

"Either massage me or go the hell to bed," Candy Cain answered testily. He poured a volume of beer down his tilted throat while his other hand held several peppermints at ready.

"I heard you bitching and belly-aching already, Ros, and I told you I'd take care of him if things worked out that way. They may not. Me and Mr. Havoc have got a large business

56 JOHNNY HAVOC

transaction to discuss. He's a man of class, that's obvious. I
sent the boys to rough him. Didn't do much good. He wouldn't
fall for a roll in the sack with you, either. So I'm going to
approach him on an intelligent level. I don't want you to
whine around and screw it up."

He administered a fatherly slap on one of her hands. It
made her yowl. Then he leaned back and grinned at the up-
side-down version of her busts which he could see from his
position. "Get me, Ros? A business man has got to separate
essential things and the superfl—the superfl—"

"Superfluous?" I offered.

"He's got a wise mouth," Rose-Edna petted, retreating with
folded arms. "I hate little shrimps that talk wise like they own
the world. They need a lesson."

"But not now," Candy Cain growled, shutting her off.

Craning his head back to normal position, he leered at me
in what he supposed was a smile. "Y'see, Havoc? I am on
your side all the way. Trying to make things painless for you.
Just how painless is going to depend on how quick we reach
the—ah—partnership agreement."

"Mind if I leave now? You're starting to talk silly."

"Silly? The hell I am!" Candy chortled, refusing to be
baited. "You're my partner."

"I would rather be in partnership with Lucifer, Atilla the
Hun and Yellow Kid Weil."

"Who's the guy in the middle?" inquired Candy blandly.
"Some Dutch gun?"

"That's exactly it. Look here, I've been worked over by
those two substitutes for members of the human race . . ."

Jalasca and Sparks exchanged dark pregnant glances.

". . . and offered ten nights in a bridal bed by your shower
bath princess over yonder . . ."

Rose-Edna Klutz glanced about for some convenient heavy
object which to throw, and luckily found none nearby.

". . . and I am slightly sick of the whole mess. For God's
sake, Cain! I'm a private citizen! I've got my rights. They
don't include being kidnapped."

"He's going to have a right to a kick in the knobs if he

don't watch his mouth," said the emotional Jalasca, tinkling the ice in his highball in a menacing fashion.

"Havoc, you lost all them rights you're babbling about when I became personally interested in you. Have a peppermint? No? Very good for the indigestion. Well, it just boils down to one thing. You might as well swallow it because you can't change it."

A growling, slightly grim note entered his rough voice. "At the moment I happen to be pressed for cash. I have been looking for means of picking up some ready change. Therefore, when Ros talked to Lorenzo Hunter during his party at The Quarter and he mumbled something to her about a bunch of papers this thick—papers that'd net him a hundred thousand clams—I became very interested. This deal happens to sound pretty legit, so I hesitate to begin throwing a lot of muscle around. Or lead either. But if it takes that to do a job."

Candy Cain put three peppermints in his jaw and snapped them in half like a trio of busted spines.

"Is that how you dragged in on Lorenzo's business?" I inquired curiously. "The party?"

"Exactly. The hick had a lot of giggle water in him. He got to babbling. Simple."

"Candy!" exclaimed Rose-Edna, wrapping up her wrapper and concealing her breasts, which had been my only source of enjoyment in an otherwise grim setting, "I wish to God you'd quit treating him like some lousy little nobleman and just knock it out of him."

"You can't do busines that way in the modern world," said Candy. "Unless it's necessary." *Crack-crack-crack.* I found myself wishing he chewed something less noisy, like fingernails.

"Why are we all of a sudden partners?" I wanted to know. "I never met you before."

"Because, little Havoc, you have the goods, the papers. I'm willing to be fair about it. I'll take two-thirds and give you one."

"Gee, dad, that's really white of you," cried I. "Phooey."

"Just what the hell do you mean by that goddamn remark, *phooey?*" Cain roared.

"Phooey. Nuts. Screw you. Go to hell. And more of the same. I need no partner."

"Oh, by God, boss! Just let me give him a belt in the family jewels," shrilled Jalasca.

"Wait!" Candy Cain raised a fat hand. "You going to be unreasonable, Havoc? You going to make me undertake the expense of an ambulance to haul your beat-up carcass out of here?"

"Exactly what makes you believe I've got those mysterious papers you're yelling about?"

"Simple, little friend. Hunter and that broad he married didn't have them when they got burned." Cain guzzled some beer, vastly pleased. "To that I can testify."

I blinked several times, becoming severely alarmed about my welfare.

"You can? That's impossible. Nothing was said about the app—the goods in the newspapers."

Edward Sparks tittered uncontrollably. Even Miss del Rio-Klutz could not supress a grin of vulpine amusement. Perhaps, I thought dreamily, if I kept them in stitches over my own seeming ignorance, they would forget about putting on the screws. I doubted it, but I had precious little else in the way of encouragement.

"That is correct," answered Candy. "Further, you marked yourself a gentleman-type individual when you refused to divulge the location of Hunter's honeymoon hideaway even when my boys almost knocked the crap out of you. But I have other ways and means, Havoc. My girl Ros went nosing around Hunter's locker—same one you looked in tonight—after I called her when the boys reported you were a blank. Ros was very lucky. She found a travel folder in Hunter's locker. All about Mohawk Mountain Lodge. I phoned, learned they were there, and me and Jalasca hopped in the bus and drove up for a chat."

"Then you fried them, huh?" I asked, a cold knot of glue forming in my belly.

With a childlike innocence whose truth or falsity I couldn't penetrate to save my soul, Candy Cain sucked one of his mints. "I did not. I arrived shortly after some other party did the job. Jalasca and me searched the place from one end to the other, didn't find a thing, and got the hell away. Don't fish-eye me, Havoc. You know a bartender saw somebody coming out of the cottage a while after midnight. If that doesn't help my story along, I don't know what could." He raised a hand. "I'm clean."

"You could have read about the mysterious solitary visitor in the daily rag," I returned.

"Could. But didn't. Shall we forget the topic of my innocence?"

Swallowing a deep breath, I shrugged. "Candy, there's nothing else to talk about."

"You're all ripe!" I snarled, leaping up. "Ripe and soft in the noggins! I suppose you expect me to rip open the lining of my coat, produce these papers you want and say it's been a privilege to make your acquaintance? I've never heard of such tactics before. Damned highway robbery even if I had the goods in the first place."

Now Candy Cain shed some of his pretense of business.

"Glance over your shoulder, Havoc," he purred ghoulishly. "Ed and Miami Joe have a couple of items which duly authorize me to take any cut of your profits I want. But lucky you'll be left with a third."

"This is the item," chortled Jalasca, waving his cannon in my direction.

With a humph, I descended again into my chair and tried to control my rampant cowardice by lighting up a smoke. I made a great show of searching for an ashtray and finally deposited the burned stub in my pants cuff. By then I had sorted out a number of notions in my head, paramount among them being the one which said that the longer I locked horns with the knucklehead opposite me, the harder it would be for me to emerge from his apartments without several leaden perforations in my flesh. I set my objective in clean, uncomplicated language: *Escape.*

Escape by the quickest possible route dictated an instant end to argumentation, a tackling around to a position wherein I might do some conning.

"All you got to do," Candy reassured me, "is cough up the papers."

"I don't have them, Candy. Pound my skull to a pulp. I still won't have them."

"Are you going to allow that little crap-head to flim-flam you?" shrieked Rose-Edna.

"Quiet, goddamn it!" Candy roared. "This is serious."

He screwed down his grizzled eyebrows and treated me to a long, hard, merciless stare. "If you're bulling me, Havoc—"

"So help me J. Edgar Hoover, I'm not. We can't do any business at all if you're so dumb you can't believe a plain, honest-to-God statement of truth when you hear it."

"He's not dumb!" protested Edward Sparks loyally. "And you shut your face, unless—"

"Will you all keep the hell quiet and let him and me work it out?" Candy raged, leaping from his reclining posture and overturning his quart of beer into a sudsy lake on the oak flooring.

Approaching and waggling a pork-chop finger under my nose, Cain rasped. "Granted I believe you may not have the stuff, but I've got a hunch you know where it is."

"This is possible," I replied with an air of disdain. "Let's suppose I do."

"Then you get it!" he barked. "Get it and give me my two-thirds or you're dead."

"Hold the freight!" I shouted. "Just one minute!"

Candy blinked in consternation. This gave me the chance to leap up and menace him modestly with an index finger jabbed in the chest.

"Do you even know what you're talking about? Look me right in the eye, Cain. Tell me what it is we're after."

"One more move, I blow off your cookies," announced Jalasca.

Risking all, I ignored him, badgering and shouting: "What is it, Cain? Don't you know?"

"Why—uh—it's a mess of papers—that—"

"What sort of papers? What's in them? Exactly, Candy? What's in them?"

In a fit of desperation, Candy Cain picked up his bag of peppermints and hurled it at me.

The sack popped and tidbits flew right and left. Candy turned purple. Then black. His shoulders shook. To his gun-toters he cried, "Burn the bastard right now!"

For no reason at all, except that my height was against me and I couldn't get their attention, I leaped up in the arm-chair and flung out my hand in his face.

"Go on, Candy!" I shouted in extremes of last-ditch histrionics. "Burn me down! And you'll never know what the papers are! Or where they are! Or what to do with them when you get them! You fat dumb crook! Do you think you just have to close your greedy mitts around them and bingo, some fairy princess changes them into a hundred thousand dollar bills? If you think that, here I am, a nice target."

Trembling to beat hell inside, I still managed to put a ferocious glare upon my puss as I shouted: "Give 'em the word, Candy! They're still a little hesitant. Fry me, you greedy son of a bitch! Then go out to a short loan company and try and raise the cash to get yourself out of hock!"

"Boss!" howled Miami Joe Jalasca. "You're in the way! He's practically inviting me to put holes in him! Please, boss, step back, just a step or two, that's all."

"Shut up!" Cain exclaimed, snagging a peppermint off the floor and pulverizing it in two seconds.

I climbed down from the chair, exhausted by my theatrical demonstrations and unsure whether they had done me any good at all.

Cain said warily, "What kind of deal you talking?"

"This kind. I walk out of here. Without any of your goons on my back. Keep tabs on me if you want. Put a creep tailing me. But stay out of my hair. You've got me dead right now, Candy, if that's your choice. But it does neither of us any good. On the other hand, when I walk out, I'll start hunting for the goods. Provided one of those dumb-bulbs over there isn't hanging on my sleeve asking a lot of numbskull questions. Then, when I find the goods, we see about the split. And it's fifty-fifty. I know the spot I'm in. But I'll set the terms. Call off the dogs, Candy. That is the deal."

"Candy, you're a maniac if you let him get away," exclaimed Rose-Edna furiously.

"Sweetie, he'll be a penniless maniac if he doesn't."

While the events of my life flitted through my brain in dismal prelude to my funeral, Candy chewed his lips, snapped his suspenders and grunted, deep in mystic thought. At last he waved in a vague manner.

"Stash the heaters, boys. He's got us, I think."

"Now you're acting like a business man instead of a boob," I said, nearly fainting. I adjusted my tie, redeemed my porkpie and glanced idly from Sparks to Jalasca. Both these worthies, considerably saddened because they had been deprived of a chance to operate on me with some hot lead, stood about in postures of despondency. I pointed a couple of fingers at them and tried to be casual:

"Which one is going to be my watchdog, Cain?"

Candy, rummaging under his easy chair for a sweet, grunted, "Jalasca can start it off."

"Then shall we understand one another from the beginning, Miami Joe?"

I approached him and gave a tweak to his view of Biscayne Bay. "As I mentioned to your employer a minute ago in somewhat heated language, I do not desire to be pestered with your unwelcome attentions. Never speak unless spoken to. Once you give me a ride back to the lot where my convertible's parked, I don't want to see your face closer than fifty yards."

Swinging around, I added, "Back me up, Cain, or there's no arrangement. I won't be nut enough to think I could cut you out once you've cut yourself in . . ."

That, of course, was sheer malarky. If I emerged from this interview alive I intended to cut him out as soon as possible.

". . . but I'm not going to have things gummed up by your professional primates."

"What the hell you mean, calling me a primate?" jeered Jalasca. "What's what, anyway?"

"Buy a pocket dictionary and look it up. Cain, you're wasting time. Tell him."

Scowling uncertainly, the sweet-toothed crook muttered grudgingly, "Do exactly like Havoc says, Miami Joe. But don't lose him, unless you want to go through life singing soprano. On the other hand, let him have his head."

Hooking a finger in his suspenders in an authoritative way and striding close so that I was immersed in essence of peppermint, Candy Cain snarled in my face:

"But don't think this gives you the right to ditch me, buster. Try it and see how far you get. If you possess any fancy ideas about ducking where I can't find you, if you think you're safe once I let you out of here, you are mistaken."

His jabbing index finger made indentations in my chest. His hot and greedy eyes glared. His slippery smile told me all at once that perhaps I was not the clever lad I had imagined. He had guessed a step ahead of me, figured the ditch, taken steps to let me know my fate would be very very lethal if I tried a dodge.

I suspected he might be right. I suspected I had not saved myself at all, but merely worked myself deeper into a large hole. Still, escaping from his presence with breath yet in my lungs, I could face the additional perils arising if—no, by blazes, when—I tried to untie his acrimonious apron strings and go my own free, sweet, larcenous way, After all, what other choice did I have?

"Candy, you're not a man! You're a lousy jellyfish!" shrilled Rose-Edna in a pet of outrage and rejection. "Didn't I tell you how he treated me? Why, if you let him walk out without so much as getting his warty little puss slapped for the way he—"

"Ah, go upstairs and read your *Reader's Digest*," sneered Candy, making it sound impossibly repellent.

I took my cue from his dismissal, avoided her poison gaze, tipped my porkpie and navigated for the double doors in all haste. I preferred to look no more upon the countenance of Mr. Charles Cain, for I had the willies just trying to figure out whether he knew I would try to abandon him as a financial partner. If I convinced myself he knew, I'd have no stomach for what I must inevitably do. And I had to have stomach for that, if nothing else, or my pockets would be empty, a fate worse than Candy himself.

Upon the street, black and deserted in the pre-morning hours, I yawned, shuddered unmercifully, slid into Jalasca's conveyance and down upon the seat, pulling my lid over my eyes. I craved rest to restore my flagging senses. In the hours ahead I was going to have a considerable task making sure my rest would not be permanent.

I issued directions to the hood concerning the parking lot, then sunk deeper on the cushions, remarking. "Just shut up. No baseball, no broads, no gab, period. Pretend you're the rapid transit driver."

That was an error. His swearing kept me awake all the way to the parking lot.

Chapter 8

AN ALARM DREW me soggily from the sack at a quarter of eight in the morning.

From my front window overlooking the bridge I could see an unpleasant, rumble-colored bank of clouds up north in the sky, threatening gloom and a deluge. I could also see Miami Joe Jalasca's heap parked directly behind my convertible at the front curb.

Dressing, I pondered. First off, I was in no position to sort out the truth or falsehood of the actions of the midnight visitors to Mohawk Mountain Lodge.

Was Candy Cain the solitary visitor glimpsed by the bartender up there, the bartender not seeing Candy's companion?

Or was the loner old Dr. Fred Willis?

And which one had caused Lorenzo and his bride to cease breathing?

A tricky little question, that. Still, it could be relegated to the background. Because one little item was, being gentle, more important.

I swallowed half a quart of orange juice and toast and

flung on my Brooks Brothers rags, thinking like a regular little computing machine.

The application, the application.

Oh, you old devil application, where are you?

Lorenzo ain't got you.

Candy ain't got you.

Gray B. Ainslee ain't got you, and man, I ain't either.

Ergo, wistful Willis, the rejected swain and possible homicide-perpetrator.

Assignment one. Find wistful W.

Yeah.

Where have you gone, Willie boy?

Rummaging through the semi-closet described by my rental agents as an expansive efficiency kitchenette, I located what I sought among a drawer of assorted cutlery and church keys, thrust the two items carefully into the side pocket of my jacket and adjusted my lid. I locked the flat door and trundled down the stairs as fast as my undersized legs would allow.

Considerably refreshed by all that sleep, I had decided to attack the matter of throwing off my pursuer with a certain sadistic flair. After all, I may be less than full stature, but contrary to what that bum Candy said, I possessed my rights and grew angered when they were violated.

Several courses stood open for disposing of my shadow, in addition to the safe course of not disposing of him at all. But this was out of the question in spite of Candy Cain's shrewd threats of what would happen if I tried.

The rear entrance of the apartment building might be guarded by Edward Sparks, but I doubted it. Candy Cain and his minions did not appear remarkably bright or thorough. Anyhow that would have been the coward's way to shake Jalasca.

Telephoning the bulls would have been the sucker's way, since my reputation with them was none too good to begin with. Telling them why Candy's lad followed me would only have brought the whole stew about the FDA application out in public. If there was one thing F. X. Magruder did not desire it was publicity.

No, the point had to come the hard way.

Skulking for a moment in the building foyer, I noted with delight that Miami Joe Jalasca appeared to be weaving and swaying at the wheel of his vehicle. I chuckled. This was going to be less of a chore and much more of a pleasure. Tiptoeing onto the pavements, searching right and left and spying no one except a broad with a poodle going the opposite way, I crept up around the hood of Jalasca's vehicle.

His snores, whistles and Morpheus-grunts sounded loudly even through the vehicle's plate glass windows. Whipping one of the objects from my coat into my hand, I paused by the right front tire, then repeated the action at the left. I circumspectly opened the door of my own convertible, released the handbrake, cramped the wheels outward and started the motor.

Fearing this would rouse the watchdog, I leaped from the seat and raced back, only to find him whistling a slumberous tune with his head thrown back against the leather.

I opened the door on the driver's side and jammed the horn ring.

"*Yiii!*" exclaimed Miami Joe, or something to that effect.

He literally sprang upward and crushed his hat against the roof of his auto. I tugged sympathetically at his coat, plucking him into the street where he tottered between rage and pain.

"I believe you're suffering from automotive difficulties, Miami Joe," said I, pointing a sympathetic finger at the front wheels of his conveyance, both tires of which were now whistling a jolly melody and deflating themselves as a result of punctures inflicted by a brace of butcher knives planted hilt-deep in the rubber.

"We do have a lot of vandalism in this neighborhood. Something should be done about these kids. *Tsch-tsch.*"

It took a moment for his plight to penetrate and his agitation to erupt. I used this interval to skip to my vehicle, slam the door and accelerate away from the curb, crying, "Do try to follow when you get it repaired. I'm going to have a very interesting day."

The sedate residents of my thoroughfare were doubtless unnerved if any of them saw a convertible racing down the street followed by a lumbering fat man with waving fists, a swearing mouth and a view of balmy Florida flapping over his shoulder. He ran a block and a half and then receded in the rear mirror, standing over a closed manhole with steam rising about him as he clutched his paunch in an agony of exertion. It made a novel sight.

I cut around a corner, whistling to keep up my courage. I had done what I should not have done. What I had no choice about doing, my insatiable greed being what it is. And I well remembered the assault of Jalasca and Sparks behind The Ego. This was a small payment. Candy's threatened consequences would be worth this little but oh so satisfying revenge.

Well, almost.

Chapter 9

THAT MORNING OCCUPIED itself with an attempted pursuit of the elusive Dr. Fred Willis, he who must possess the big, fat and valuable Nirvana application.

First off I telephoned the UPI works in Industrial Flats from a seamy pool hall. I got connected with Magruder, received an authorization and a promise of bodily harm if I failed him, then was transferred to the company personnel department.

They presented me with the address of Dr. Willis' bachelor apartment. I had a miserable drive through the fumes across the river, succeeded in jimmying the door of the Willis place, and set about a methodical search. Not that I anticipated turning up the Nirvana item, but at present I had no leads whatever. The police, certainly, had searched the apartment ahead of me, yet I opened all the closets even though I didn't imagine Willis would be anywhere about.

He was not. On the other hand, a writing desk bore a leather-framed photo of a mousy-appearing broad in shell-

rim glasses which was autographed *To Freddie, Love, Sis.*
Oh, yes, Havoc thinks of everything.

Except simple connections like relatives.

One more phone call to the UPI factory confirmed that Dr.
Willis had no kin living except the number in the photograph,
her name being Miss Constance Willis, her residence a street
back across the river in the Lincoln Heights section of the
city.

This struck me as a juicy lead, scratching as I was for anything at all. With lightning speed I memorized the address,
mounted my convertible and charged back to the clean city,
where one could breathe pure, sweet carbon monoxide again.

Lincoln Heights, up north, was a pleasant, woodsy district
characterized by the size of its building lots. The apartment
houses were set two feet apart, a reckless excess which would
not have been tolerated downtown. I located the number of
the Willis sister's dwelling, a two-story affair, and saw by the
mailbox that the lady occupied the top floor. The bottom
was in possession of someone or something called Crudgeford.

Ringing the top knob, I got no answer. I tried the lower,
got an answer and wished I hadn't. The beefy who came
lumbering into the vestibule weighed all of three hundred
pounds.

"No aluminum pots, no greeting cards, no vacuum
cleaners with attachments for removing body ash from the
mattress, no magazines, no plastic dishes, no ten cent insurance policies, no encyclopedias, no cosmetics no foundation
garments, no nothing!" cried this harridan, plucking bobby
pins from her mop of wild hair at a great rate and menacing
me with her large torpedo-shaped bosoms. I cowered under
her glance and tried to smile fetchingly.

"Are you Mrs. Crudgeford?"

"No, I'm Governor Rockefeller's wet nurse. Who in hell
do you think I am? Any little bastard of a salesman who
comes around here bothering me right in the middle of
today's episode of *Life's Lavender Path* is going to get his
block knocked off."

"You've got it all wrong," I responded, flashing her my
wallet and the star which I had won from a vacationing Great

Falls, Montana, deputy police captain in a crap game. Before she could wonder why the star said Montana and showed a couple of beeves grazing, I thrust it away and announced, "I happen to be a private investigator looking for Miss Constance Willis. Now if you're the landlady of this place and she's not home, as apparently she isn't, you'd better just trot out your key and let me in."

"Investigator?" the female Crudgeford muttered. "I would think the poor dear had talked to all the police she could stand."

Life's Lavender Path forgotten, some of her truculence vanished. Apparently she decided I might have an exotic background.

"This is a private matter," I snapped. "Now, where's Miss Willis?"

"Why, working at the Lincoln Heights Branch Library!" replied the Crudgeford, slightly more cowed each second as I increased the fierceness of my gaze. Trying to placate me in my role of stalwart of the law, the shrew leaned over with her bosoms knocking around in her bathrobe and simpered secretively, "The dear thing has a lovely position there, you know. Assistant chief librarian as well as being in charge of all cataloguing."

"Fascinating," I remarked, visioning Constance Willis as even more drudge-like than the bad photo in her brother's apartment presented her. "Mrs. Crudgeford, I haven't got all morning to stand here and discuss your tenant. I intend to wait for Miss Willis in her apartment." I wasn't sure whether I did or not. "And if you refuse to let me in with your passkey, then I'll simply have to exercise my rights and kick the door down."

"Oh, my God, No!" cried the overweight person. "I just had the hallway painted three weeks ago. Stand right there and I'll get the key and take you up."

So saying, she disappeared into the entrance to her own apartment, from which issued several plaintive and tinny sentences informing me that Sibi Brackswater had ostensibly shot down Gregory Fer de Lance, thus placing herself on trial for murder while her unknown stepchild Tad Tompkins went without shoes at the county orphanage. *Life's Lavender Path,* right enough. I was getting interested when the Crudgeford returned with a jangling key ring and heaved herself up to the second floor, unlocking the door to the apartment in a highly illegal fashion.

I oozed myself through the portal and wedged it closed upon the curious matron, who was crushed not to be able to watch the law at work.

"That will be all, thanks. I'll knock on the ceiling in case I need you."

"Oh, good God, don't do that. The whole building was entirely re-plastered four months—"

I dismissed Mrs. Crudgeford's construction problems by closing the panel in her map.

Then I ranged the four-room apartment from front to back, through the living room, the lace-decorated bedroom, second bedroom with wall bookshelves crammed with paperback novels—sheer heresy for a librarian—and ended my tour by lifting the lid of the laundry hamper in the bathroom.

Miss Willis was not secreting her elusive brother in the hamper, nor in any of the rooms or closets, that I could tell. As I dropped the hamper top with a bang, I thought the apartment must possess a remarkable echo until I realized the front door of the apartment had slammed.

I fumbled my way into the short hallway, rushed forward and clamped my mitt over the mouth of the new arrival.

"For God's sake don't scream!" I exclaimed.

Constance Willis closed her molars on a couple of my fingers, which I promptly released. Then, vibrating with fury, she flung off her woolen coat and began to stalk the living room.

"Why in the name of heaven would I scream? Mrs. Crudgeford could hardly wait to tell me there was a policeman waiting. Look here!" she said furiously, spinning around, "If you've messed up my things, I'm going to telephone the police station and report you. I've done nothing these past few days but talk, talk, talk to your confederates. I'm slightly sick of all the questions and insinuations. Now, just when I think I'm finally getting a small share of peace and quiet, what happens?

They send you over here to invade my privacy. I'm not going to stand for it a minute longer!"

"You . . . you . . ." I gargled. "You . . . are Constance Willis?"

Fortunately, instead of remarking that she had some connection with Governor Rockefeller, she simply nodded her head, sweeping off the shell-rims at the same instant.

Miss Constance Willis, wearing high heels, must have stood exactly five feet.

In addition to that, she had such juicy proportions thrusting out this way and that beneath her tweed skirt and white-collared sweater that I doubtless presented a lascivious spectacle for several moments. The photographer who snapped her for brother Fred had certainly long since gone out of business, all thumbs. Any man who could transform this finely-constructed, dark-haired little wench into the drab ghoul in a leather frame I'd looked upon with disgust should have experienced bankruptcy long ago. I left a peculiar stir among my ductless glands. My yokel stare made Miss Willis all the madder.

"Must you stand there and leer at me?" She whirled around, turning her back and ending her sentence with a slight, saddened catch in her tones which brought me to my senses. "Of all the detectives that have paraded in here, you're certainly the worst."

"Hey! Hang on, Miss Willis. Don't get so upset. In the first place, I told the old bi— the landlady downstairs that I was a private investigator, not regular policeman."

"That's all I need! Clever private detectives!" she fumed, stamping around to face me once again.

She had deliciously red, ripe lips.

Deliciously sparkling blue-gray eyes.

Deliciously large, plump, well-pointed— This would get me nowhere.

"What are you going to do with me?" she inquired. "Beat me with your flask of whiskey?"

Through her mockery, I coud spot a genuine vein of weariness, even bitterness, ill-becoming to a chick so pleasantly assembled. Trying to show her I wasn't all boor, I removed my porkpie.

"What I told Mrs. Crudgeford was also a fib. I have no state license as a detective. The name is John Havoc. I'm a guy who works for other people on assignment basis. Not detective work, exactly." I'd figured the only method of getting her to my side was candor. "At the moment I'm personally employed by Thomas Magruder, board chairman of UPI. Your brother's company!"

"I have told the police," Connie Willis replied steadily, "and I will repeat to you, Mr. Hammock, or whatever your name happens to be, that I do not know what's happened to my brother. I have not seen him, I do not know where he is. If he's hiding, I don't know why, and I don't know where. I'm well aware that the police think he had something to do with the murder of that musician and that despicably, witch-tongued Magruder girl. But if Mr. Magruder sent you here to try and make me admit Fred killed . . . Fred killed . . ."

She bit her lower lip, snatched up her purse, found and nervously lit a cigarette.

". . . his daughter, then you might as well leave. I know Fred wouldn't do anything of the kind."

"Magruder, frankly, isn't interested in who frie . . . er, killed his daughter, Miss Willis. He is only concerned with recovery of the Food and Drug Administration Application on that tranquilizer, Nirvana. Your brother's project."

Rapidly I sketched a few of the details of my first interview with F. X., naturally painting myself as an operative called in by Magruder himself, but altering little else, and not even deleting a hint of the situation featuring Charles (Candy) Cain. I tried to watch her eyes during the recital, instead of other luscious features of her person, and toward the end, as I wound up my gilt-tongued con in a burst of oratory, I thought I detected half a smattering of belief in her expression. Pressing on, I cried fervently:

"Believe me, Miss Willis, I can't do a thing about it if your brother is hung up on a murder charge, even if he didn't do it—but if he's fooling around with the application, I think I can square it."

Daring all, being a double-damned fool, I added:

"I am positive I can square it. F. X. and I—"

I showed her how we were. Then I placed my porkpie upon my head. "That is the conclusion of my speech, Miss Willis. Doubt it or not, it is gospel."

"I . . . I don't have the slightest notion about Fred's whereabouts," she began, making a nervous show of examining a small gold watch on her wrist. "Even if I did—" The gray-blue eyes sparked. "What makes you so certain Fred would even have the photostat of the application in his possession? After all, maybe he just got so mixed up over that worthless Magruder girl that he wanted to go off by himself for a little while."

"Possible," I countered softly. "Yet the application is tied in with the whole business. Lorenzo Hunter and his, ah, wife had it at one time. Or knew where to get it. They did not have it when their bodies were found. Nor does that unpleasant gentleman I mentioned, Mr. Cain, know its whereabouts. Gray B. Ainslee, the one working for the South Bend clan, has not seen it, but he knows it exists. Therefore, unless we are all chasing an imaginary nothing, someone is holding the joker right now. And people don't get blas—I mean shot over papers that don't exist. Who murdered whom, who took the application from which when, I can't say. I only thought that your brother was the last remaining choice, barring intrusion of a party none of us have met. I don't think there is any party of that type in the wings." With a sigh I finished, "The answer I get is Dr. Willis."

"And I told you once, Mr . . ."

"Havoc, if you please. John Havoc, boy—"

"Oh, don't try to be amusing, not now!"

She averted her gaze. I swallowed in a flustered manner. I had pushed her almost to the edge of tears, and could have kicked my own dumb butt for it. Her words became more fraught with effort, punctuated by small dry sobs.

"I want to be free of this whole horrible mess. I can hardly stand talking about it. Freddie's the only family I have in the whole world . . . and I . . . I know he's not guilty of any murder."

Then she stiffened, whipped about and blazed: "But even if I could pick up the telephone and call him this minute, I wouldn't, not to turn him over to you."

"Then what else can I say?"

I reached for the doorknob and paused dramatically.

"I admit I must look pretty shifty, breaking in here and hunting for him the way I did. But let me repeat. Nothing I can do would clear him of a murder rap. The other part of the deal I might be able to arrange. And I would do it," I blurted like some stricken swain. "By God, I would, if you—"

Tapping her watch and close to tears, Connie Willis said, "You'll excuse me, please Mr. Havoc. I'm allowed only an hour for lunch. I must be back at the library at one."

Saying that, a peculiar, frightened flicker darted into her gaze. I didn't grasp it, but it stopped me cold and started me thinking. All of a sudden I would have taken on oath that she was keeping something from me. Minutes earlier I had been prepared to believe her tearful story. Then the break in her acting ability hit me mallet-fashion. I didn't know.

"Here," I said, dragging a card and pencil from my pocket and scribbling down the phone number of Sven-Anton's station at Twenty-Two. "If anything develops—I mean, if you should hear from your brother, explain that I want to help. Then get hold of me at this number. Ask for Anton and give him the message."

I extended the card, but Connie Willis would have none of it. So I laid it atop her thrown-down coat, unable to keep my hot-blooded gaze from her face and frame. Like fun I was looking for a sign that she hadn't been telling me the truth. I was looking for, or at, much, much more.

"Must you stand gawking like some kind of sex maniac?"

"Excuse me. In my business I don't meet many nice-looking chicks I can look straight in the eye. When it happens, it's somewhat overpowering."

Gargling foolishly, I banged into the edge of the opened door, righted myself and muttered, "Good morning, Miss Willis."

Life's Lavender Path, or a reasonable copy thereof, was blaring through the closed door of the first floor flat as I descended. I heard the clicking of a lock and hurled myself out onto the pavements under the lowering gray sky.

Thunder rumbled way off. Marching along to my convertible, I scraped my loafer toe on the cement like a lovesick mope.

Oh, what a face. Oh, what a build. Why must you eternally pursue the dollar, Havoc? Why must you place yourself in such positions, meeting a lovely chick just the proper size for — just the proper size, and then wind up in her sight nothing more than a creature wrapped in a label decorated with skull and crossbones, clearly marked with a noxious six-letter word beginning with *P?*

It nearly reformed me on the spot.

Chapter 10

FOLLOWING THE EMOTIONAL jimjams I'd experienced in the presence of the staunch-breasted Miss Constance Willis, a pensive mood overtook me.

Indulging it, I reclined a while behind the steering column of my bus, puffing a weed and trying to decipher the flash of guilt I'd noted on the chick's face at the point when she mentioned returning to the library by one.

My watch indicated only thirty minutes to wait. Without precisely having a reason for doing so, I snapped on the motor and started a cruise to the end of the block, where I would, I'd decided, wait and see whether the chick actually went back to her place of employment, or fled in another direction instead—to Freddie, maybe?

Congratulating myself upon my cleverness, I did not notice the inhabitants of the dark auto until I drew practically abreast of it.

The vehicle occupied a parking slot half way between Connie Willis' building and a tobacco shop on the corner. Seated inside was a party with a fedora upon his head and a second party wearing a dark blue cap to which a legal-look-ing shield was affixed.

Plainclothes behind the wheel flung me a cursory look as I tooled past. I wrenched my neck half out of place to prevent them from looking at me square. It took every smidgen of will I possessed to keep from pushing the gas pedal through the floor, sending me thereby out of their presences at ninety or more. With fits and pants I muffled the nerves I always get from law enforcement personnel, pulled to the curb at the corner with trembling digits, adjusted the rearview mirror and tried to appear an innocent soul parked outside a nicotine shop.

Despite no desire to be spotted by the blue laddies—I didn't recognize plainclothes in the heap, but I knew damned well more of the minions knew my map than was true of the reverse—I'd still reasoned instantly that if they bothered to watch Connie Willis' abode, I could do no less, perhaps with profit. I ought to be able to put an eye on twice as many de-tails a copper could spot. Oh, sure.

Ten minutes to one.

Overhead the gray sky boiled with all sorts of ominous clouds. Thunder crackled and whacked frequently. A motor growled down the throughfare.

I spotted Connie Willis marching along the pavements half a dozen yards behind my car and lurched deep beneath the wheel as though fumbling with my shoe. I had no desire for another interview at the moment.

I conked my head on the wheel post getting up again. During this interval Connie Willis had turned the corner past the tobacco shop. One last glimpse gave me a picture of a large paper sack clutched under her arm. Harking back to my juvenile days, the words *lunch sack* gonged in my head.

Whereupon I recalled that the firmly-hipped Miss Willis had been preparing to eat at home when I left. Now, what could that—

I suddenly found myself peering straight into the face of the minion with the shield-decorated cap. He floated past my window as the unmarked car tooled slowly in a cornering curve, off in the direction of the lady librarian. This official soul continued to stare at me through the back window until the police wagon went out of sight.

I examined me in the rear mirror.

"If you have anything but rocks upstairs," I instructed myself, "you'll make an illegal U-turn and get your ass and your automobile far, far away."

This was sound, logical reasoning. I promptly proceeded to turn on the ignition, lock in the automatic stick and take off down the boulevard one block behind the cruising law-bus and two behind the pert bobbing figure of Miss Willis and her paper satchel.

A block from the gray stone of what must be the library my attention was momentarily distracted by a crowd of adolescent loungers, all tight levis and leather coats and Vaseline-pomaded ducktails, hooting and jibing at the vanishing prowl car.

This seamy crew, a good two dozen of them, milled on the sidewalk in front of a dismal establishment identified by a creaky tin sign as Pops Zybysko's Sweete Shoppe. I was fortunate in snatching this moment of identification, for just as I passed, several of the lads, in a spirit of wholesome merry-making, hoisted one of their number on their shoulders and the agile little wretch pulled the tin sign off its moorings and chucked it at the back fender of my car.

All of them hooted uproariously. The spectacle grew even more interesting when I noted that a prisonlike structure occupied the other side of the street opposite Pops Zybysko's. Carven letters on its lintel announced: LINCOLN HEIGHTS PUBLIC TRADE AND INDUSTRIAL SCHOOL. At an upper window I spied a jolly frosh throttling one of his mates with a window blind cord.

Since school was theoretically in session at one in the afternoon, I assumed the mob at Zybysko's to be graduate incorrigibles. Glancing in the mirror, I spied an old gent in an apron come rushing out from the Sweete Shoppe to retrieve his sign. The last I saw of him, the youthful company had raised him up, hurled him in the street and were pelting him with old fibreboard milk cartons and Mars Bars wrappers.

So bemused had I been by this spectacle of rampant adoles-

cence, I'd completely forgotten the chick for almost half a
minute. I found myself in the next block.

Directly behind the library stood a brick one-story light
manufacturing joint. The Hidden Charm Brassiere Works,
according to its front billboard.

A rear door on the gray stone pile, opening on the alley
next to the bra shop, was labelled: KEEP OUT, LIBRARY EM-
PLOYEES ONLY. Nowhere could I spot Miss Willis or the legal
sedan.

I U-turned in the alley, swung and parked before the shop
of the bosom-builders. I strolled along the side of the library
to get a better picture of things. I began to have a little sneaking notion about the whereabouts of Wily Willis. Why had
his sister packed a fat paper sack for her return trip?

My plan called for a survey of the front of the library, to
be followed perhaps by a frontal assault through the main
doors.

Stepping around the corner to the front of the library, I
made my initial error.

The Lincoln Heights Branch fronted upon a well-forested
park a block long through its middle. The park itself, and
surrounding street, took a circular shape, avenues radiating
off the concrete at the various compass points. A solitary
bum slept upon one of the benches across the way but otherwise not a soul enjoyed the woodsy pleasures of this city oasis
paid for by everyone's taxes but mine. No doubt the graying
heavens and the mutter of thunder kept the sun-takers in-
doors.

But it did not prevent other souls from being abroad upon
the pavements, namely the two inmates of the prowl car and
a third plainclothes type, all grouped together for a chat at
the park fringe across from the rising steps of the public book
vault. The one in uniform saw me a second after I saw him.

Plainly they were staking the place. I made all types of odd
motions, trying to find a packet of matches in my pocket and
re-light the weed in my mouth, blown out by the wind. Instead of turning sharply and retreating, I tried to look like an
innocent citizen.

The match packet flipped out of my hands. I tried to catch it, dancing for a moment like a ballerina with St. Vitus.

Bemused by this sight, which called more attention to my person than I wished, the uniformed minion tugged at the elbows of his companions and pointed at me. The third plainclothesman, evidently the proprietor of the gray auto parked behind Uniform's wagon at the park curb, swung to give me a lamp.

And there I danced, willy-nilly trying to catch my matches, while I caught clear sight of Detective First Grade FitzHugh Goodpasture.

Upon several occasions I had chanced into his presence downtown. A six-foot cigar-munching individual, he knew me by sight and reputation. Coincidence could not have brought me to the Lincoln Heights Branch Library in broad daylight, his official noggin must instantly be reasoning. I gawked for an unspeakable half-second, my arms upraised in a loony position to catch the matches even now wafting away down the gutter under a snappy breeze.

Detective Goodpasture growled a syllable to his companions. All leaped from the curb, hammering shoe leather at a rapid pace, straight for me.

The shock of it all unnerved me. I turned full about and began to walk for my heap. My thoughts were fevered.

Exactly how far would I get, invading the library with them standing about watching me?

Could I draw them off, divert them?

Perhaps I'd done it by my very appearance on the scene.

But if I wanted to come back to the library I would have to draw them off first, get them interested in me.

How could I get back if they were so interested they kept following me all the time?

Oh, mother.

Hard soles slapped at the corner a short way behind.

"Havoc, damn it! Stand where you are!" floated the voice of Detective FitzHugh Goodpasture upon the breast of the breeze. "Want to talk, you little—"

Presently I arrived where my convertible occupied a curbspot outside the walls of Hidden Charm. If I leaped in, they'd be on my tail in a shake and a half. Desperately I searched for means of eluding them.

I noticed a dank-looking areaway past the bosom works running back between the manufacturing concern and an adjacent apartment. Halting for a gulp of air at this mysterious opening, I gave FitzHugh and his companions a clear shot at my path. Then I plunged in, hoping there would be more than a dead brick wall at the end.

When I reached that end, it was blessedly un-blank. I gained ten seconds on them.

The uniform had apparently stumbled and sent his fellows clambering all over the limbs of one another. I could hear Detective Goodpasture's cries of alarm and consternation rising unprintably to the gray sky. A window flew up in the apartment and a shrewish voice wanted to know who was using all that goddamn foul language.

I plunged to my right and banged off a light pickup van. When I righted myself I took a quick breather. This alley intersected the one behind the Lincoln Heights Branch in a T-shape. I could either run back down the alley in the direction of my convertible or pursue the same direction by entering the deliveries door of Hidden Charm.

I chose the latter. FitzHugh's crew had untangled itself and was half along the stone passage between buildings.

One, two, three, up a flight of iron steps, running like hell straight into the large bay-like delivery entrance.

Congratulating myself on having grown five feet one inch and therefore somewhat lighter of foot than flatties like Goodpasture, I neglected to see the stubble-chinned youth emerging from the rear of the bay carrying several fibreboard cartons in his arms, the whole lot stencilled with silhouettes of dolls wearing nothing but bras. Head down, legs and arms pumping, I struck him *kerplang.*

"Jesus M. Christ!" cried he.

One of the cartons dropped off, giving me a grip on the lapel of his hickory shirt.

I swung him about in a full one hundred and eighty degree swing and sent him racing like a juggernaut to the edge of the loading platform.

Just above its rim popped the heads of Goodpasture and his staff, all brandishing their weapons. The hapless youth wavered on the brink, then fell with a *yipe*.

Several of the cartons cracked open as the delivery lad rained his person and his parcels upon the heads of the lawmen.

Brassieres flew every which way, blown by the wind. In a fit of fury Goodpasture swiped at one of the devilish items which had gotten its straps around his ears and its cups across his eyeballs.

Having only a fleeting glimpse of this novel sight, I raced on into the bay, bumping against a wooden pallet-skid piled high with more of the blue-stencilled cartons. It required but a moment to tip over this pallet, setting a few more seconds' worth of obstacles between me and my pursuers. As I plunged through the doorway into the body of the factory itself, Fitz-Hugh and his squad came charging over the box barricade, tumbling and falling this way and that, Uniform sporting a D cup at his belt like an extra set of handcuffs.

A hallway flanked by open green steel racks of boxed bras led forward to what looked like a work area, brilliantly lit and drowned in the clatter of a hundred sewing machines.

Pelting forward in this direction, I whammed against a portly woman in a smock just emerging from a sign-marked area identified as housing LATEX STUFFERS A THROUGH D.

Skidding, I grabbed for support. I lurched off the frame of the fat cursing jane. In doing my macabre little dance for survival I discovered that the green steel racks, though rather wide, were not firmly anchored.

One of the racks bearing boxes of Latex stuffing on its shelves began to teeter.

"Watch out, Mother!" cried I, dragging the cow by the scruff of her smock, pulling her from under just as the rack swayed, tottered and clanged over in the corridor.

I imprisoned Goodpasture and his lads in a maze of uprights. Boxes and cartons slid and flew. Lids dropped off. Contents rained out. These contents served to inform me that Hidden Charm made not only legitimate bust-housing but dishonest ones as well. Goodpasture, the other plainclothes and Uniform were inundated in a tidal wave of pink rubber cones.

Uniform, with a strangled cry, tried to batter a path out of the rubber chaos. In attempting to step over the obliquely-fallen storage rack, his hand closed on another, as mine had done. Further cups of larger size began to rain.

"My God, there goes another one!' screamed Goodpasture, just before he disappeared beneath several thousand of the things.

Pressing onward, inflamed by my success, I cast aside the spluttering and obese forelady and concentrated on reaching the cross-aisle at my end of the manufacturing room.

Drawing nearer, oblivious to the clang and batter of the coppers disentangling themselves from the fallen shelves, I saw that the chamber ahead housed some eighty or ninety sewing machine tables, each manned by a smocked dame, the whole crisscrossed with moving belts.

Various of these laboring females snagged bits of cloth from containers whizzing along the belts. Then they jammed the bits into the machines, basted, stitched and assembled them with a whir and a hum of electric treadles. Then they flung the finished undergarments into other cartons travelling on still other belts. The whole bedlam was overlaid with the shouts and exhortations of several foreladies and the constant ringing of a frenetic gong, doubtless intended to incite the workers to a frenzy of speed.

It took me an instant to decipher a path through this wild series of assembly lines. Eventually I picked out a long concrete aisle running straight down between two banks of machines. Those on the left had placards above them labelled TEAM C. Those on the right were identified as TEAM D.

Pelting madly along this concrete thoroughfare, I was hardly noticed. The lady workers attacked their machines like mad creatures. Apparently each team competed with the others. All sorts of jolly profanity flew back and forth as I whizzed along. Salvation was in sight, however, in the shape of pastel-hued double doors at the end of the aisle.

"I hear Team C is running four B cups behind this morning," jeered a member of Team D as I raced past. This statement was accompanied by much raucous merriment from others on the team.

It produced considerable antagonism in Team D further along the line. A kindly, rosy-cheeked grandmother, silver-haired and sweet, called out from her machine:

"Ah, blow it out, Gussie. You got lead feet and that ain't all that's lead."

Half-way between the cross-aisle where I had entered this clattering sewing room and the double doors which led, I hoped, to the street, I screwed my head around in mid-stride for a peek behind.

Detective First Grade FitzHugh Goodpasture was lurching among the sewing machines way back at room's end. He was still brushing rubber bust cups off his shoulders, crying something about Stop That Man! Uniform and the other plain-clothes had not come into sight, but old FitzHugh was lumbering along like a bear.

All this I noticed in the half-minute my dome was cracked around. Consequently I failed to spy the forelady pushing a wheeled truck stacked high with finished cartons of garments. She was proceeding across my path at a furious pace, shoving the cart like a dragging hotrodder. In the moment just before collision I heard her exclaim hysterically:

"Tell that Gussie she's full of bullola! Here comes a double batch of B cups from Team C, six minutes ahead of sched— hey, you little bastard, look out!"

I struck the rolling cart amidships, knocking it into a sharp left turn.

The forelady dumped against the head of one of her Team C workers. All the accumulated goods representing Team C's six-minute advantage flew off over the heads of the laborers. The rolling cart, accelerated by my bump, preceded me along the aisle, a juggernaut out of control, weaving erratically.

Someone on Team C attempted to trip me. I punched one of the lovelies square in the puss when she dove out after me in a flying tackle. A cry of triumph went up from FitzHugh Goodpasture, intermingled with shrieks of rage and ringing gongs.

Suddenly the double doors at the end of the aisle batted

inward. Three gentlemen in shirt sleeves boiled into the sewing room. They reeled back at the sight of finished garments flying through the air, the sight of me charging them behind the cart, the sight of Team C lunging across the aisle and falling upon Team D with feline cries as pointed pump toes kicked shins and elaborately-painted fingernails got mixed up in other ladies' hairdos.

"Oh, for God's sake," came Goodpasture's frustration-wracked cry. "Ladies, ladies! I'm a police officer! Let me through! Let me through, by Jesus or— Madam, kindly keep your hands to yourself! Dammit, let me through!"

Taking in performance but a tenth of the time it requires in narration, my journey along the aisle was completed now through three-quarters of its length. However, the grimmest obstacles yet loomed ahead, in the persons of the trio of executives who formed a flying wedge at the double doors and pointed grimly at my approaching figure.

Since I was the stranger nearest to them, they hastily identified me as the cause of their production difficulties. One sprang to the wall, cracked open a glass case and, swearing furiously, came up with a large fire ax which he brandished in an attempt to bring the pandemonium into control. The other executives ducked their heads in menacing fashion and prepared to give me lumps when I reached them. That would be in another moment or so.

Redoubling my efforts, I leaped out with long short-legged strides. I kicked my soles on the concrete for redoubled momentum. At the same time I heaved myself aboard the runaway cart.

Clutching the handrail, I hung on to this engine of destruction and shouted to the executives that they had better get their butts out of the way, for the aisle floor, I discovered with a trace of panic, sloped ever so little. The freight was picking up speed down the grade.

With cries of horror, Fire-Ax and his mates rushed out of the way.

Whammo, right through the double doors went the escape express.

Through another aisle in a smaller room where a couple of

fashion models were posing against a backdrop of a Roman coliseum, under glaring lights and in front of a bulky camera.

The models shrieked out frantically and covered their under-garmented torsos. The photographer gave a strangled cry.

That's all the scenery I saw on that part of the tour. The cart banged through one more pair of double doors and hurled into a marble-floored reception library.

Straight ahead stood a desk. A secretary's back was between me and it.

I cried for the shorthand girl to have a care. She glanced over her shoulders, she screamed.

She scrambled to safety just as the cart bonged the desk and skidded it half-way around. I had a vague glimpse of several salesmen, equipped with attaché cases, leaping to their feet in panic. But I desired to see no more, choosing instead to fling myself from the cart and down the short stairway, banging off glass doors and emerging with heaving breast into the street.

My only hope now lay in FitzHugh Goodpasture still being embroiled in the riot between Teams C and D. I jumped into my convertible, gunned the motor and went zooming away, describing a continuous S-curve in the street for several moments.

At last I recovered control of my racing senses. Crowds of youthful adolescents scattered along the sidewalk at Pops Zybysko's Sweete Shoppe as I thundered past.

Zip, I turned a corner, nearly ran into a bus, dodged it. *Zip*, another corner.

I pretzeled a path through this side street and that for five minutes. Then I slowed down to a normal speed of sixty-five. No pursuing engines showed in the rear glass.

Feeling considerably shaken by the whole experience, I tooled slowly back to my district of town. The sky had turned a handsome black shade to match my mood.

Unless all the signs proved wrong, a wild storm was abrewing. But it could be no worse than the storm which I had roused with yours truly as the center. Entering the Hidden Charm Bra Works, I had intended only to elude the demons of the law, not engage in inciting riots and wholesale property wreckage.

As if I didn't have enough to worry about with Candy Cain steamed up because I'd pulled a ditch! Now Detective Goodpasture would be seeking my scalp with a vengeance. And all for a miserable ten thousand clams.

Why, this kind of mental torment wasn't worth that. I might have been maimed, riding the bra wagon through those series of banging doors. Were I smart, I'd telephone F.X. Magruder and tell him to let Sturns take over, then quietly surrender to the constabulary and live out my days in the peace of the penal farm.

Ten thousand bucks wasn't . . .

Havoc, cried I mentally, have you no wits? Are you so easily cowed?

Will you abandon the cause of those millions of souls beneath five feet six inches who seek endlessly for a champion, some half-pint to prove that small stature need not be equated with small accomplishment?

Think what Candy Cain's bunch did to you. Don't you want to give them lumps?

Think of how many pairs of Adler elevators a man could buy with ten thousand dollars. Although I would not have been caught lifeless in a pair of elevators, it was a point.

Even though the worst was definitely yet to come, for ten grand a guy can take a hell of a lot. And then some.

Chapter 11

DESPERATELY DESIRING A few moments of snooze in the comfortable confines of the double sack in my flat, I stopped instead at a drug emporium and swilled three cups of black coffee. Then I proceeded to the downtown.

I surrendered my convertible to a lot attendant and sought refuge in the smoking loges of the nearest motion picture palace. Returning to my diggings beside the river would be hazardous enough once night has descended, but sheer suicide during the daylight hours. So I enjoyed a couple of weeds and watched a youth on the screen leap from his Cushman motorcycle and do battle with a werewolf lurking in some bushes. I went to sleep at the point where the werewolf was choking the life's breath from the adolescent while the heroine of the epic, clad in a leather coat with a bloody dagger for a crest, squeaked pitifully in the background.

It being a triple feaure, I awoke refreshed to find the werewolf back on the screen choking the adolescent. I hung around until the victim kicked off, then wandered into the street and consulted my wristwatch.

Slightly past seven.

I wolfed a frank and an orange at a corner stand, wished for my raincoat against the few drops beginning to patter from the rumbling night sky, sought a phone booth and dialed Twenty-Two.

"Any messages, you old fraud?" I asked with faint hope.

"As a matter of fact, yes," replied Sven Rasmussen, doing the bogus Lugosi bit. "Only a few minutes ago, when we were opening. A young lady, who would not give her name."

My spirits began to inflate, then drooped.

"Not that crazy Spanish teacher I had in there last week? I was a damn fool to give her the number. That bimbo wanted service night and day. Give me the worst," I continued, hardly daring to hope.

"Not that one, no," Sven returned with a sigh of dismay. "That one I know. Heavens, what appetites in one so small. This lady gave no name. She said she wished to discuss your offer. I can imagine the sort of offers you have been offering," he added archly.

"It's not what you think at all," I answered hotly, almost wishing it were. "Any instructions from the wench? Or am I supposed to contact her via telepathy or something?"

"I couldn't say. However, she informed me that she would wait for you from eight until ten this evening at Einstein's Espresso Shop. Do you know where that is?"

"Down where all the boys and girls wear beards and leotards. Yeah, I know."

Suddenly my better sense called a halt to my aroused enthusiasm. This might possibly be a well-coached Rosalind del Rio extending bait. No need to bother Sven with such dismal projections, however.

"Thanks for the answering service. Anyone else been around after me? Like for instance members of Candy Cain's scout troop? Or police types?"

"None. Ah, John, one second before you hang up—"

A somewhat somber note crept into his tone.

"All evening, while we have been setting up, some word of unhappy rumor has been circulating among the waiters. As yet I haven't had a second to check upon it. But I did hear Heine mention Cain's name. My boys have very sharp ears, especially for things that happen in the seamier quarters. Perhaps you'd like to telephone back after you have some espresso? Perhaps it is nothing at all. On the other hand, if you are having dealing with that bad man Cain and there is activity . . ."

I said unhappily, "I like it not. See if you can dig up the gist of it. I'll either jingle or walk in later tonight."

"You should be in a decent, safe profession like being a headwaiter," he advised.

"What? And get poked in the chops by outraged members of the Four Hundred who can't get a table? No, thanks, good old Sven. Me for the underworld."

And with this I shut off the conversation, wishing fervently I felt as blithe as I pretended to be.

What was Candy Cain up to? If lots of folks knew it, it might be large enough to spell another, worser jam.

Maybe Sven Rasmussen had a point, I reflected, guiding my convertible through a patter of raindrops down toward the arty part of the city. I would have made a nice floorwalker. A good encyclopedia salesman. A crackerjack manufacturer of yo-yos. I could not see myself in the role of a corpse at all. *Boom bang*, went the thunder in the black sky, laughing.

On a dim thoroughfare where a misbegotten Michelangelo was taking his canvases down from a board fence under the threat of impending downpour, I located the Einstein Espresso Shop, a narrow institution filled with clouds of smoke. I loitered awhile on the pavement, looking for such types as Sparks and Jalasca among the bohemians, then suddenly knew I should have had more faith in the good old race of human beings and the cockeyed forces which guide it.

Scrunched up at a rear table over a small cuplet of Mr. Einstein's hell's brew, bundled in her wool coat and wearing her shell-rims for a screen—Constance Willis.

I felt something of a freak entering the bohemian bistro, attired as I was in a normal-type shirt and tie. Beneath the boiling clouds of smoke from little brown cigars and the hiss of the chrome espresso machine, I was branded a philistine by cutting looks from the anemic assortment holding court at the tables.

I stepped around a little lady in turtleneck sweater who was tapping ecstatically on a pair of bongo drums while her male companion performed a handstand on the floor beside her. Both were reciting in Japanese.

Another chin-bearded inmate was painting a cubistic mural on the forehead of his coffee-partner.

Cross-legged upon a table at the rear of the chamber sat a party in a turkish towel loincloth and a beard that came to his bellybutton, constructing some sort of abstract doodad from an opened cylinder of Tinkertoys.

A bimbo with a book stood up and exclaimed, "My libido is inundated by Pepsi-Cola."

Then she sat down. Several persons applauded. One threw an espresso cup at her head.

The rotund proprietor, M. Einstein, caught it on the fly and smiled at the tosser, exclaiming, "Sonofabitch!" in a joshing way. A number of the habitués told M. Einstein what he could do. Among the alternatives offered were moving to Suburban Meadows and taking up residence in the board room at United States Steel.

I took out a chair and plunked myself across from the beauteous Connie Willis just as a folk-singer leaped on the table, whanged his guitar and began to serenade us with a tune about Zeus and a goose riding a caboose on the Ozark

Railroad. I felt I was either the world's squarest man or a visitor to the funny farm, or maybe both. I concentrated on Connie.

"Good evening," I said for a starter. "Got the message."

"Here you be, Mr. Babbit," exclaimed Einstein, setting a cup of espresso before me. "My compliments. From you, no money. Take the gospel of true existence back to the savages in the jungles of Book of the Month Club Land. *Pax.*" He grinned and floated off.

"Quite a joint," remarked I.

Connie Willis kept glancing toward the curtained front windows in a nervous manner.

"It—it was the most outlandish place I could think of. I imagined it might be the safest, too. And I didn't really believe you'd come, Mr. Havoc," she went on, treating me to an unreadable look with her blue-gray eyes. "Until the moment you walked in the door I thought it might be just a trick, that you weren't really working for Magruder but for the police, or—well, I don't quite know what I thought, except that it was bad. I apologize."

"Accepted." I scalded my intestines with espresso acid. "But I hardly expected a bite for the bait so fast. I didn't plan on it at all, matter of fact. You told me you didn't know where your brother was hiding."

I let that dangle suggestively.

Constance Willis could not be so simply suckered.

"I didn't tell you I knew."

"You telephoned me, pretty. That means you wish to discuss your brother's welfare. You could hardly undertake such a palaver not knowing anything about his circumstances."

Flushing a little, biting her lips, she nodded.

"Oh, all right. You caught me there." Then her gaze blazed. "But I'm not telling you a thing about where Freddie is right now until I find out what sort of an arrangement can be made. I—I talked . . ."

She hesitated.

"Go on," I replied, feasting my lamps on the contours of her coat. "I won't bite. Much."

Ignoring the implications of my remarks, Connie pushed

her cup aside and locked her fingers together on the tablecloth, leaning forward.

"I talked to Freddie today. He's terribly frightened, Mr.
Havoc. He's done something wrong and he knows it. But he
doesn't know what to do about it. He can't really prove he
had nothing to do with the murder of Lorenzo Hunter and
that—that Magruder beast. And yet . . ."

With a determined sigh, she gathered her courage and
blurted softly: "Freddie went up to Mohawk Mountain Lodge
the night of the murder. And saw them both. Alive, Mr.
Havoc. He left them that way."

Trying to ignore the blaring folk music, the burden of
which was that Aphrodite in her nighty had transferred at
Little Rock and boarded the Texas and Pacific and was
working on the section gang running a race with a jack-
hammer, I grew exceeding bold and laid my hand atop
Connie's.

There was a crackle and a crash, hormonally. Connie's
eyes flashed a moment, then grew ashamed. This was no time,
that glance informed me, to indulge herself.

With the ardor of a boy scout reading a spicy novel on
the back shelf of her library, I wondered what she'd be like
when she did indulge. I had the impression she'd be pretty
blinking good. Stifling these base emotions, I gave her hand
a brotherly, uncle-ly squeeze.

"Better take it from the top, okay?"

"How much do you know about Freddie's—relations—with
Shirley Magruder?" she asked me, drawing her hand back
as a hot tinge of pink mounted the column of her throat.

I shrugged. "He fell for Miss M. She didn't reciprocate.
He was shook when she spliced with the guitar-player. How
this fits with the Nirvana application—dunno."

"It fits perfectly," was the reply. "Perfectly enough to
make Freddie into a blind fool. Oh, he realizes it now. That's
part of the trouble. He can hardly stand the humiliation of
it, in addition to the real trouble he's gotten himself into.
I didn't learn about this until poor Freddie came to me looking for a place to hide. But I'm getting ahead of myself again.
I'll go back.

"About the time Shirley Magruder decided to marry that Hunter person, she approached Freddie with a sad story about how her father had cut her off without a cent. Everyone at UPI knew Magruder couldn't stand the girl. Freddie figured this was a natural happening. Shirley, of course, neglected to tell my brother that Magruder had cut her off because she was planning to marry Hunter. I imagine the old cheat—Magruder, I mean—just used that as an excuse to get rid of a millstone."

"Bang on the nose. He did."

"The short of it is this, Mr. Havoc. Shirley said she needed money in the worst way. Freddie's salary just wouldn't be enough. After all, if they were going to see each other from now on . . ."

With a little pout of disgust, Connie shook her head. "Can you imagine how it affected poor Freddie? Here he'd chased Shirley for years, always too shy and bookish to do more than give her a peck on the cheek. Then suddenly she was promising him all kinds of—of forbidden delights."

"Those forbidden delights are murder," I said, imagining some of my own.

"Please don't joke with me, Mr. Havoc. Freddie was seduced without imagining that True Love has floated in the window. Shirley said she knew a man who'd pay a hundred thousand dollars for a photostat of the FDA application on Nirvana. Think of what they could do with that money! So poor Freddie, who would probably have fainted away in other circumstances if someone ever suggested he'd sell out UPI, filched the application overnight. He got a copy made and presented the copy to lovely little Miss Magruder. The next day she called him on the telephone. She informed him that she appreciated his gesture but that she was marrying Hunter."

"A nice minx," I commented, pouring more espresso into my heaving intestine. "I can understand why her father didn't much care when her life was lethally terminated."

A small sad nod again from Connie.

"Poor Freddie was frantic. Certainly he'd be marked as the guilty one once Rx Corporation got on the market with a product like Nirvana. He was bound to be suspected since he was the group leader on the project. Freddie told me the one thing that goaded him to action was the fact that he knew he'd admit the theft if someone asked him a direct question about it. He's that kind, Mr. Havoc. A sweet, shy, dumb young man who got most of what he knows about life from a biology text."

"His predicament is apparent," I murmured sympathetically. The folk-singer's ballad was running on endlessly. Currently Hercules in his BVD's was riding the rods of the Atcheson, Topeka and Santa Fe. Mr. Einstein and the lout with the cubistic mural on his forehead were performing an impromptu ballet to the music's strains.

Trying to shut out this beat cacaphony, I leaned across the table and prodded gently: "Freddie went back to Mohawk Mountain?"

"He followed the honeymooners' automobile from City Hall after the wedding."

"I didn't notice any tail on their bus. But then I wasn't watching for one, either."

"Mr. Havoc, you can't imagine how frightened my brother was. He nearly had a nervous breakdown just going into a sporting goods store and buying a blank cartridge revolver. He wanted to buy a real one, but couldn't bring himself to do it. Anyway, he hung around the lodge until a little after midnight. The bar closed. Lorenzo Hunter and his new wife reeled into their cottage. Freddie had brought along a pint of bourbon. He must have been nearly blind. He couldn't have done it sober. But he was sober enough to march into the cottage and wave that bogus gun and demand to know where the application was. Hunter and his lady friend got panicky. It turned out they had the document in their suitcases. Evidently they were planning to sell it and then leave this part of the country. Freddie took it. He ran out of the cottage, got scared when he noticed someone watching him from the front door of the lodge—"

"The night bartender," I put in.

"I suppose. He went home, opened his newspaper in the morning and saw the story about the murder. Up until then he'd been ready to go to Magruder and admit the whole mess, even if it meant his job. But he'd been through so much that the killing pushed him over the edge. He came to me, begged me to hide him until he could leave the country. I told him he had nothing to fear—I mean in the larger sense—if he turned himself in. At least I told him that initially. Now I don't know."

Her blue-gray eyes probed me like a blade. "Freddie did not kill them, Mr. Havoc. But there's no way on earth to prove it. He has no witnesses, nothing to support—"

"No way to prove it," I broke in, "unless we get the genuine culprit to admit the deed. That culprit, I'm beginning to suspect, may be the Mr. Candy Cain I mentioned. A sneaky sort. Capable of double homicide. Sounds more capable than Freddie, at least. I must admit, though, that he also declared in strongest terms that he didn't trigger them."

"Which one of us do you believe, Mr. Havoc?" asked Connie Willis intently.

Covering my discomfiture by slopping down the final unholy dregs of Mr. Einstein's potion, I muttered, "I'd sooner believe you and your brother, Connie. I am going to proceed on the supposition that your story—and Freddie's—is true."

Trying to screw my map into my really, really serious expression, I added in somber tones, "We are all going to wind up in the pokey unless I do go ahead and conduct my business on the basis of Freddie's tale being true."

"Business?" Constance Willis shied, upsetting her empty cup on the tablecloth. "If you've got some plan up your sleeve for putting Freddie in more trouble, I promise you—"

"Don't chew my head off, please," I protested. "I want to help your brother. I want to help you, too."

My suggestive intonations were met with a half-hidden flash of her eye. Oh, mother. She knew how to play a tricky deck, right enough. Without saying a word, she had suddenly informed me that I might be rewarded with more than a thankful shake of the mitt. This doll, I mentally opined, is not all Dewey Decimal System, not by a country mile.

Maybe when it was over, if it was ever over and I remained in a single piece, she might even enjoy bestowing tangible evidence . . . well, at least her eyes put it so, unless I'd lost all ability to read the signals of the opposite sex.

Harrumphing to conceal my dismal little lusts, I rushed on: "Item one. You apparently know where your brother is hiding. Do you think we can reach him? I mean, without making a public carnival of it?"

"I'm certain we can."

I masked my thoughts, hoping not to reveal that I had already guessed about what treasures might be hidden somewhere in the Lincoln Branch. I did not wish her to think I was too shrewd, or she might shy. Pressing forward, I said:

"Then does he have the application copy with him right now?"

"He does. Mr. Havoc!" she said, alarmed. "Where are you going?"

"Sit calm and try to trust me. I'm going to put a buzz to F. X. Magruder."

"Magruder! Oh, no, Mr. Havoc, that'll just wreck—"

"It'll wreck nothing. In fact, it might just solve some of our problems. If there is one thing Magruder wants, it's return of the application. I think he'd ransom his own granny to take the Nirvana thing from circulation. Now, sit here."

I summoned M. Einstein and bade him bring the lady another cup while I ran out to renew all my subscriptions to Luce Publications. Curling his lip, he left. I bent over Connie's shoulder, kneading it to give her comfort.

"You have trusted me, pretty, and you must do so again. At least until I trundle back from that wall telephone at the rear of the hall. We may be out of this pretty quick, if you just give the maestro his head."

"All right," she responded, convulsively squeezing my hand, causing all sorts of imbalances in the outpourings of my glands. Her moist lips glimmered in the smoky light, and once more she promised that if I were a good lad . . .

"I'll trust you."

As I marched through the motley throng to the wall instrument, I was not convinced that the maestro deserved to have his head given him, but after enduring the rigamarole of abuse F.X. Magruder heaped on me for waking him, I felt my optimism had not been unjustified. Fifteen minutes—eight of them being occupied with profanity from the board chairman—later, I returned to the table and slipped in my place with a Cheshire look on my puss.

"Success, madame. I've tamed the roaring lion."

Bending forward over the table cloth I plunked an index finger in my palm. "Dear old F.X. still harbors considerable resentment against your brother. But not enough that it can't be wiped out if the application is safely returned."

Briefly I outlined the nefarious plot to transmit a phony application via Ainslee to Rx.

"As to how the return of the application affects Doctor Fred, Magruder swears there will be no prosecution. I think he can be trusted. He's crooked as a snake when it comes to sapping the opposition, but unless I've misjudged him, he'll keep his word once he gives it. Of course I wouldn't put too much faith in your brother's chances for advancement at UPI. In this category," I finished smugly, "I elicited a further promise from F.X. in which he'll guarantee your brother a good letter of recommendation should he wish to change jobs. Under the circumstances that might be advisable. At least Freddie won't be finding a new position with a criminal charge marked down on his personnel chit."

"You're right," Connie exclaimed happily. "Oh, that's perfect, perfect!"

"Swell!" cried I. "Let me telephone Ainslee, the passer-to-be of the bogus application, and together we'll hop in my convertible and go pick up brother Freddie."

"No."

Quick, decisive bobbings of Connie Willis' head put a sudden clamp on my feeling that I had seen an end to the grim business.

"You'll have to give me a few hours to present the idea to Freddie. Oh, Mr. Havoc, there's nothing I'd rather do than get Freddie out of hiding this very instant. But I know the state he's in. He won't make a move now unless he takes time to think about it. He's very much aware of the price he paid for hasty action on Miss Magruder's wedding day. I know he'd stay in hiding, miserable and frightened, for the rest of his life, rather than jump at something that might frighten him off. I'll have to go to him alone. I'm sure he'll do it. But you must believe me when I tell you that he's terribly wrought up. I don't want to throw away all you've done. Please. Does it make so much difference? In the morning—"

"Many dark and dreadful things could happen between now and morning," I cut in, jogging my memories and reminding myself to check back with Anton on Candy Cain's sudden activity.

It made me extremely nervous, the prospect of wasting precious hours between now and daylight. I was about to mount a further argument when Connie Willis spoke up quickly:

"It can't help but come out right, Mr. Havoc. I feel it."

"You and Doctor Peale," I remarked. "Always on the bright side. Oh, hell, have it your way. I suppose I'm just inventing trouble."

Slapping an artificial smile upon my map, I patted her hand again.

"You see brother Freddie post haste. I'll telephone you early in the morning and we can collect the goods. Agreeable?"

"Oh, yes, Mr. Havoc. I—I wish I could tell you how sorry I am about the way I spoke to you this morning. You've done so much for Freddie already. I wish—"

She did not inform me of the nature of the second wish, but a sudden pressure of her fingers upon mine completed the sentence nicely.

I snagged my porkpie from a wall hook and stepped over a couple of lads playing chess on the floor in the aisle beneath several of the tables. I presented Mr. Einstein with a dollar bill. He refused it.

"Give my regards to the *nouveau riche,*" he said, "and tell them their idols have feet with Dr. Scholl's corn plasters on them. Then I shall be repaid." With a mystic smile he laid a hand athwart his chest. "*Pax,* oh child of the benighted middle classes. Blessings upon thou whilst thou undertake the return to Cubesville. Long live planned obsolence and General Motors Corp."

"Crazy, dad," I replied, giving him a middle-class wink and shagging my fanny out of there.

On the sidewalk Connie Willis waited for me, turning up the collar of her woolen coat. Gaudy flashes of lightning blazed and fumed. A garbage can rolled past in the street I expressed the view that we would soon have a ring-tailed storm.

"Let me drop you at your place, huh?" I concluded, steering her elbow. She shied a little, drawing away.

"No, there's a taxi stand on the corner. I'll take a cab. It'll be easier."

"Easier shmeasier, Miss Willis. I sense the absence of complete and utter trust. I swear and cross my bleeding heart I will not follow you, nor try to learn the whereabouts of brother Freddie until he has decided to join our cause."

Holding up my right hand palm forward, I suddenly realized I was telling her the gospel. I wouldn't follow her, when every larcenous instinct told me I was screwy not to do it. Lord, the tricks those ductless glands play. You'd of thunk I was a member of the Beaver Patrol.

"Thank you, Johnny," whispered the suddenly warm Miss Willis. "Thank you!"

Before I could say help, the staid and stacked and my-size librarian had flipped open the front of her woolen coat and barged up against me on the deserted windy street.

She flattened my back against the brick wall next to the espresso shop. One of her hands came up and around my neck. Her breasts and hips made contact, all points swaying.

She inclined her head to the side and mashed her mouth against mine, hot and tasty and wide-open. I recovered myself, plastered a couple of hands on her firm rump and further solidified the kiss with a mighty hug.

Her hair blew in my face, tickling my nose. I was practically ready to let us both be blown down the street on the crest of the storm without a care. Whatever she had learned at the Lincoln Heights Branch did not include the naughty manipulation of her pelvic region. That came strictly from Nature's urges.

When at last we unclasped, she flung me a last hot, penetrating look and then dashed off toward the cab stand while I straightened my lapels and called a "so long" after her small running form.

When her taxi had pulled away I let out a yip and conked my knuckles against the bricks in sheer exultation.

Perhaps I'd been too gloomy of late. I felt like the devil's own ring-tailed wonder boy at the moment. I would have waited until Methuselah's funeral for poor Freddy to make up his mind if it were required. Whistling, I flung into my convertible with happy abandon and merrily took off for Twenty-Two.

"Many guns," announced Sven Rasmussen, twiddling a menu. "Many very bad guns."

"For God's sake, you fraud!" cried I. "Stop talking like the Sioux chief in a Buck Jones flick. Tell me what it's all about. You have picked up facts about Cain, no?"

"Some unhappy facts about Cain, yes."

Sven became Anton and gave me the sort of regretful shake of the head reserved for patrons whose position on the social scale entitled them to nothing better than the smallest table in the darkest corner. At some other restaurant.

We stood in the momentarily deserted main floor foyer of Twenty-Two, my convertible double-parked in the street, motor running while the doorman kept an eye for wayward patrolman in return for a five-spot. I had skulked into the plush spot after much studying of the street in both directions, seeing ultimately neither Sparks, Jalasca & Company or representatives of Detective FitzHugh Goodpasture. Now I almost regretted having been able to enter the club so easily. Detained on the outside, I would not have had to endure the mournful, even funereal expression on Sven's dour face.

Clucking and sighing, the black Dane continued: "If you are engaged in any activities with Candy Cain, I'd suggest you bring them to a swift conclusion. Preferably through the method of buying an airline ticket to Tibet. Candy Cain doesn't like someone. Candy Cain is doing something about it."

"Is this a veiled reference to those many guns of a moment before?"

"That it is, John lad. The waiters, chiefly Heine, scouted the clientele. I myself phoned a number of less swank bistros. As you know, the city includes a dozen or two freelance guns, not affixed permanently to any of the mobs. According to what mournful tunes came to my ears, Cain is purchasing them at from three to five hundred dollars per head. For what assignment I cannot guess. Perhaps he has rats in his flat. He's the kind of bum who can only think of hired hoodlums for any difficult job. But if their objective is human and, ah, should happen to be around five feet in height . . ."

"Five feet one inch," I mumbled, thinking fast. "These guns are being bought right now?"

"Several have already been purchased. Others are still being added to the task force."

"No rumble about for why?"

"Not a murmur. Hey!" he said abruptly, losing all traces of his ersatz Continental dialect. "I could hide you in the wine cellar a couple of days—"

"I have nothing to fear," I said fearfully.

"Don't feed me that baloney. The manner in which you turned green just a second ago indicates you're up to your wily little throat in whatever is behind Candy's quest for additional arms. Hell, you'd be comfortable down there among the magnums."

"No, Sven. Thanks all the same. Comfortable I might be. But also impoverished."

I gave his hand a shake to show him I appreciated the tip. Summoning a gay and carefree laugh to my lips, I chaffed, "Don't worry. Fore-warned means fore-armed."

"Ridiculous. It simply means you can make your own funeral arrangements ahead of time."

With many a mournful gasp and sigh over my fate, he removed himself reluctantly and went to give attention to a leading producer of films just sweeping his scarlet-lined operatic cape from his shoulders. The color of that lining

—a shade this side of fresh plasma—only served to increase my apprehension.

Oh, Havoc, why in hell's ding-dong damnation couldn't you forget glands and concentrate on greed? Why couldn't you sell out and follow Miss Willis when you had the chance? So nothing could happen overnight, huh?

In a fit of nerves I wedged myself into a telephone booth and emptied my pockets until I came across Gray B. Ainslee's phone number. This I dialed. Momentarily his vaguely southern voice responded.

"Havoc, Ainslee." I talked fast and quietly. "Hang around the talk box early tomorrow morning. Be ready to hop in your bus. I think I may have Willis and the goods pegged down. If so, I want you there. We're going straight to UPI to get the dummy made. I repeat, do not leave the vicinity of your telephone. Got that?"

"I do, I do, and it's a distinct pleasure to hear from you, old partner. Before you go, would you mind telling me how you accomplished this little miracle? I'm mighty inter—"

"I'm glad. Just keep listening for that jingle, Gray B."

Whack, I hung up and re-stepped into the foyer.

Sven had disappeared with the film mogul. I went outside and half down the high stone steps, turning up the collar of my jacket and putting my porkpie at an angle to drain off the rain which was now beginning to fall in earnest.

I ducked and scooted for my convertible, calling thanks to the doorman. I put the gear stick in drive and eased forward out of my double-parking spot. I planned to try sneaking past any guards that might be stationed at my dwelling. And then try snatching some sleep.

All of a sudden I noticed an unusual spectacle. Back along the street three autos turned on their lights and roared after me. Candy Cain's army had already been recruited, outfitted and trained. It was now out to conquer its first objective.

Me.

Chapter 12

Do MORTICIANS EVER conduct funeral processions during the hours between sunset and sunrise? This I wondered, guiding my convertible unsteadily through traffic.

That must be it. Why, it can't be anything else. Some citizen has floated off the sphere and is being interred. That would certainly explain a trio of vehicles rolling along behind me in brazen parade, nose ornament to rear bumper.

Rain pelted the windshield of my bus. The wipers wheezed with a bad case of pneumatic asthma. Laughing in a light-hearted manner, I poked a weed into my face and stoked it with the dash lighter. Why, what in the name of Christmas had ever caused me to imagine that Candy Cain's hired hands would be so open about their pursuit? No hoodlum in his proper mind would allow his troops to act with such a noticeable lack of guile.

If the vehicle on my tail were not the occupants of an unusual cemetery procession, perhaps they belonged to a bunch of contestants from a quiz program. Quiz program contestants were always getting involved in all sorts of merry stunts. Like driving around town on a rainy night riding the bumper of people named Havoc, scaring the bejesus out of them.

But Candy Cain? Fiddlesticks. No hoodlum in his proper mind . . .

Candy Cain had lost his mind.

I whizzed the convertible into an alley, cutting to the next through street, and the three automotive bears whizzed right after me.

"And I could have cashed that life insurance policy and enjoyed a cruise around the world before I went," I remarked, jamming down the gas pedal and making a break for it.

I'll grant that no matter how wretched the shadowing tactics of Candy's paid bullet-pushers, they drove expertly. For six minutes I made geometric high-speed traffic patterns up, down and around neighboring streets while the cavalcade stuck mercilessly on my tail. *Boom, bang, boom,* went the thunder. What a miserable night to end it all.

It was not a question of losing them in traffic. As the watery downpour increased, the traffic lessened until it seemed there were only four Detroit products moving in the whole damned universe. I did my best to eliminate from my head all fuzzy and inane excuses about midnight interment processions of strange cults and quiz program stunts involving autos, and settled down to the grim task of saving my own bacon.

The chasers seemed in no hurry to curb me. They could easily have done so if they desired. Malicious bastards, I thought, spinning around a corner and heading generally back toward the river and my flat near the bridge.

That immediate section of the city I knew very closely. Perhaps a way to ditch them would suggest itself. It damned well better had, or they'd drive me out of my nut playing cat-and-mouse this way. One of them, the closest vehicle, even sounded a jeering tootle on its air horns, to invite me to enjoy myself while I still had breath to do it.

Of course I could try surrendering, try conning my way out of Candy Cain's bad graces a second time. I doubted that would work. Thus I arrived on the rain-washed thoroughfare upon which my apartment building fronted.

All heavenly hell was cracking loose, lightning every other minute and thunder in between. The Mississippi River floated down one gutter and the Nile down the other. My collar became damp with perspiration. I slowed, approaching the front of my building. Behind me the mechanized murdercade did the same.

Staring blankly through the dripping windshield and scrounging for a bacon-saving idea, any bacon-saving idea short of suicide or the white flag, my eye lit upon an oddly familiar sedan parked at the curbing. It faced the opposite direction from which I drove. As I spattered by, my tires raising a tidal wave, I let out a small yip of exultation. Behind the wheel of that sedan rested a black figure with a peaked head.

Now, if that peaked head had a shield on it, and some other inhabitants of the unmarked squad car happened to be waiting . . . But cripes, they must be waiting! A uniform wouldn't be parked all by his lonesome, would he? If he would, I was cooked. But now I thought I had a chance.

With a hoop and a holler and a tromp on the fuel pedal, I zipped left at the corner. Left again down the rear alley. Braked with an excruciating squeal in the middle of a small lake.

Hopping out hock deep in the wet, I whizzed down the areaway between buildings as auto doors began to slam behind me, ker-*chop*, ker-*chop*.

"The little crud went in that passage there," a voice yammered over the rain. The lethal horde sounded like a dozen buffaloes moving through a water hole.

I passed the flat's back entrance and arrived at the iron fire stairs which I proceeded to climb. Up the face of the structure in the pouring rain. Making as much noise as possible. My soggy hands fumbled in my soggy pocket for the key I'd need, quick, if I ever reached my floor in one unit.

Flash went the lightning. I gazed down with a wrench of the gut to view at least ten ugly, mean-wrinkled maps charging up the iron in pursuit. Several large-caliber bullet-shooting devices winked and gleamed.

A light or two began to pop on in various apartments in the different levels of the building. Bleary inhabitants peered into the storm with angry expressions, wondering why the cross-country track meet had gotten mis-routed up the side of their building.

My chest ached. A corn throbbed on my small toe. One flight more . . .

"Can't I blast him in the behind?" floated a savage and throaty cry from below.

"You know the orders," sounded the sandpapery answer. "And quit—*oof*—stepping all over my rutting shoes before I haul off and baste you in the teeth. There he goes!"

There indeed he did go, whamming around the last turn, skidding on the iron and rescuing himself at the final moment before his momentum pitched him over the rail of the landing.

Bouncing back ball-fashion, I levered the brass bar which operated the fire door and pelted into the service corridor. A vaguely familiar inmate of the same floor, all curlpapers, bathrobe and a crossword puzzle book in one hand, blocked my path with a truculent expression.

"If this is some sort of wild party, I'm going to get the manager on the telephone and demand that your lease be cancelled."

By this time I had reached a cross-corridor. I heard the clang of the fire door opening and the roughened tones of a gunsel:

"Ah, put a slug in the old bag's fanny if she gets in the way."

Miss Crossword Puzzle shrieked piercingly. I blessed her for it. If that could but rouse the minions I hoped were waiting eagerly for me . . .

No time to think. *Whap*, I fell against my door. I got the key in the back lock by a miracle and crashed into the dark kitchen.

With the cool sureness of the plainsman tracking game through dark woods, I fell against my efficiency refrigerator, yanked it open and grabbed the first thing I could find. A quart of milk.

Slamming the door of the icebox while booting the apartment door shut behind me, I heaved the milk bottle at the ceiling willy-nilly and heard the ceiling fixture go *crash*.

Dodging gracefully to avoid the shower of milk and tungsten filaments, I flipped the back lock just as a number of burly bodies contacted the panel forcefully and broke the top hinge. I spun around.

"What in the name of God is going on back there?"

shouted a voice I recognized as that of Detective First Grade
FitzHugh Goodpasture.

I sprang from the kitchen to the living room. Some soul
had just switched on a floor lamp. In the momentary gleam
I spied old Goodpasture leaping from the sofa where he'd
been waiting in the dark. His plainclothes companion from
the bra works leaped up similarly across the chamber.

One quick look was sufficient. They had blood within
their eyes. All mine.

"By Christ! We've been just waiting to get our hands
on you!" Goodpasture lunged.

"The barbarians are coming!" I exclaimed, wrenching up
the floor lamp, yanking its cord clean out of the socket
and darkening the chamber again.

Wood splintered in the kitchen. I flailed about with the
floor lamp. FitzHugh Goodpasture cried out in an extreme
of suffering as I brained him a glancing blow.

"Sorry," I muttered, but it was all lost beneath the
further destruction wrought by the flying, swinging floor
lamp. I connected unerringly with all three of the other
existing lamps in the room. Then I heaved the floor lamp
through a front window just as the door from the kitchen
became crowded with heavy shapes outlined against the
back hall's glow.

"What the rut is he doing?" cried a voice. "Has he flipped
his wig?"

"There he is in the corner," came another exclamation.
"Christ, he's growed!"

"Just a God damned minute!" roared FitzHugh Goodpasture, lumbering from the shadows.

More reinforcements began to crowd the kitchen. They
thrust members from the front of the ranks into the living
room. The small space rapidly became remarkably crowded.
I got down on my knees and scooted among milling feet
as members of the pistol mob cried for lights and Goodpasture wailed, "By God, I'm a police officer. I demand to
know—"

That, friends, combined with the lamp I threw through the front window, surely did it.

"Police! Jesus T. Christ!" came a scandalized scream from one of the shooters. "Get them, guys, but whatever you do, don't use the rods. Somebody light a match!"

"Just a minute, you!" FitzHugh panted. "Stop shoving me. I'm an officer of the—"

"No guns, no guns!" chorused the crooked element. "You know what they do if you shoot a cop. Hey, damn it, somebody get a match going! Who hit me in the crotch? Take that!"

"Hey, Moe, for God's sake, what you trying to do? It was a accident!"

"You ain't Charlie, you're one of the rutting cops! The place is crawling with them."

"You're under arrest!" FitzHugh Goodpasture howled plantively. "You're all under arrest!"

The demolition of my belongings commenced at that point.

Articles of furniture began to fly through the darkness as friend fell upon friend in a bedlam of panic-sparked antagonism.

A match was lit. I glimpsed a hired gun throttling a bulb-nosed person that certainly wasn't a policeman. Then the match went out.

I crawled tactfully behind an easy chair, moving in the general direction of the rear door. Someone sat or was thrown into the chair, thereby squeezing my head against the wall.

It was pretty mortifying. The repair bill would stagger the House of Morgan. I might get evicted. But I did have a chance of escaping with most of my skin. I wrenched my head loose, determining to make the most of that chance.

Without warning the apartment's front door flew from its hinges. The officer from the auto downstairs leaped into the fray, doubtless summoned by the lamp I threw out.

Half-way upon my circuit of the baseboards, everyone shouting, everyone tangled and taking pokes at his brother in the confusing light which filtered from the back and

front hallways, a criminal type was punched in the stomach
and sat down upon my head.

I got him off by an unceremonious employment of my
digits. I crawled forward while the victim exclaimed, "Is that
you, Sherman? You sneaky punk! I always knew you were
out for me."

The unseen and angered soul triggered a shot into the
plaster where I'd been crawling a moment before. This
produced further wails from the leader of the gangsters, to
the effect that the hot seat awaited those with quick trigger
fingers. Simply beat the crap out of the bulls, wherever they
were, and let's get the hell away.

The speaker was then apparently kicked in the shins by
an individual known as Big Swede, who straight out got his
lumps. Ahead I could smell the freedom in the spilled-milk
kitchen.

The uniformed person from below-stairs blew his whistle
and continued to blow it. Reaching at last my sought-for
goal, I lurched up on my feet, skidded through a pool of cow
liquid and headed for the rear hallway.

"In one minute I am going to start firing!" came
Goodpasture's strangled warning.

"Pardon me, folks," I panted, bulling through the crowd
of tenants assembling outside my door. Foremost among
them was the lady I'd met before, brandishing her crossword
puzzles.

"He's the ringleader!" she cried. "It's some sort of orgy."

"Can't we call the police?" a man piped up. "We'll probably
all be killed."

"The police are in there!" I heard Crossword shriek.
"The fix is in."

"I'll bet it's some kind of St. Valentine's Day massacre
engineered by City Hall."

Leaving the outraged and terrorized tenants shuddering
on the fringe of the din, I belted around a corner onto the
storm-whipped stair landing and went downward pell mell
as fast as my short legs would stump.

Even standing safely upon the pavement at the base of the

building, the din rising into the night from my floor was frightful. I ducked along to the alley and took a moment to raise the hood of the first gunsel car parked behind mine. I lobbed the distributor cap over a fence. I did the same wiith the caps on the remaining pair of conveyances, then wasted no more time and gunned away from the scene of the holocaust with a wall of water rising up behind my tires.

The storm had gotten so fierce I could barely see to drive but I went close to fifty out of the alley anyway, damning the cost.

Oh, greed. Oh, the things it makes you do. A pair of pedestrians recoiled, drenched, as I dragged away from the alley mouth. I yelled through the windshield: "You haven't even begun to know what difficulties are."

It just seemed, the harder I tried, the worse it became.

Had I But Known, as the lady novelists write. By all the greenbacks at the mint, H.I.B.K.!

Chapter 13

NOT IN A long while had I witnessed such a display of rain and electricity as descended upon the metropolis once I got shed of the bedlam in my apartment.

I was forced to navigate my convertible in mid-street all the way downtown to prevent its being swamped. Once arriving in that deserted locale, I drove up on the high ground of an empty parking lot, stuffed a dollar bill in the pocket of the attendant snoozing in his wooden shed, helped myself to a stub and ran around the corner to a bar, where I consumed several Scotches.

Instead of bracing up my soggy constitution, the alcohol rendered me hazy and dull. But I had a number of hours to hide until I could contact Connie Willis for what I hoped would be the last move in this outrageous and mayhemic game we were playing. I needed a place to go. What cozier, more secluded nook than the smoking loges of my favorite all-night picture palace?

So I went, and sank down with a snore just as the were-wolf throttled the motorcycle youth still another time.

The city seemed afloat when I staggered out at fifteen minutes past eight in the morning, having overslept to a nearly disastrous degree. The storm had ended, fortunately. My dampened garments began to dry as I sat in a drugstore and swilled half a pot of coffee. Then I rushed to a telephone cubicle, inserted a dime and rang Connie Willis' number.

"What number were you calling, sir?" responded the operator with chilling formality.

"Why, the number I looked up in the telephone book, lady. Lincoln Heights eight, four nine six nine. Kindly return my dime and I'll try again. It's very impor—"

"I am veree sorree, sir," said the operator happily. "Due to the severe storm last evening, all telephone service in the Lincoln Heights district is temporarily interrupted. The repair crews are working and the damage should be remedied in a few hours."

"How about the Lincoln Heights Branch Library?" I exclaimed, slightly alarmed. "Don't sit there and tell me I can't call that either. This is an emergency."

"I am veree sorree, sir, but due to the severe storm last night, all telephone service—"

"Thanks an ever-loving heap," remarked I, denting the receiver whilst I slammed it down.

This kettle of finned things I liked not a bit. It should prove to be nothing more than a temporary interruption to my scheme for completing a hazardous assignment, yet it struck me as a rotten sign, though just why, I couldn't exactly say.

I claimed my convertible and set out at a snail's crawl through the swamped boulevards. The time already stood at twenty minutes before nine. Under normal conditions I would have made it to Lincoln Heights in time to catch

Connie Willis either at her apartment or on the way to the library to make her nine o'clock opening hour. But I was beginning to believe that I was not normal, and I knew damned well my conditions weren't.

I arrived at Miss Willis' residence at fifteen after nine with moist brakes and a gloomy mood. Parking around the corner from the tobacco shop, I sulked under the awning and scrutinized the pavements leading up to her domicile.

Nowhere did I see a conveyance resembling a police bus. Maybe the bulls had given up on her. But the real truth, which I suspected, was even more chilling.

Detective First Grade FitzHugh Goodpasture had temporarily diverted his attention to another target. Which target I needn't say. I merely got the prison willies just thinking about it.

All would be lost if I chickened now, so I tramped on foot to Connie's building. I expected shrill cries of apprehension to issue from each areaway I passed. But no official enforcement persons were about. Reaching the vestibule, dimly suspecting that no Connie would be present either, I peered about the mailbox for some sign or message she might have left. I nearly jumped from my loafers when the lower door banged open and Mrs. Crudgeford emerged.

"Mr. Hassock?" she inquired, dimpling at me in a fetching way.

"That's Havoc, and no, I'm not selling aluminum cookware. I was looking—"

"I know, I know!" she responded secretively. "For Miss Willis. She had to run along to the library. Very conscientious little dear. But somehow she discovered that our telephone service was out of commission. She asked me to give you a message, if you should happen to drop by."

Her mascara-muggy lamps grew circular. "Oh, she seemed quite anxious that I deliver the message to you. Most disturbed. I've never seen her—"

"Enough social intercourse," I leered. "Give me the communication, kindly."

The Crudgeford simpered. "All she said was, Ten this morning at the library."

With a sigh of relief I summoned enough kindness to thank her. "I understand. And now—"

"Tell me!" cried she, seizing my garments. "Is there something between you and Miss Willis? I mean, she's such a little person, and you're—well, I certainly don't mean to offened you, but if all this passing of messages means a rendezvous or something, you can count on me to keep your little secret. I think love and romance are so—so glandular, don't you? Every morning on *Life's Lavender Path* . . ."

I abandoned her, bubbling, in the vestibule. Time for glands when the pigeons had gone home to roost at Industrial Flats.

Hoofing swiftly to the corner, I entered the tobacco shop and accosted the wizened granddaddy on duty among the filter-tips.

"Tell me, sir, how far it might be to the nearest telephone in working condition? I understand you can't get a call in or out of Lincoln Heights. It's rather pressing that—"

"No need go bab like that, sonny," he answered in puckering tones. "You just drive straight on down that there street out in front until you cross the railroad tracks. You'll find yourself smack dab in the Millwood district. A customer of mine told me this morning they didn't have no difficulties with the dials in Millwood."

"How far might that be, if you don't mind telling me?"

"You planning on buying anything, or you just after some free advice?"

"Well, I wasn't planning to buy—no, hang on."

I snatched up a copy of the largest of the morning dailies whose headline had caught my attention. I flung the gent seven cents across the glass counter. "Now how far?"

"I reckon it about a mile. Five minutes, depending on whether you're one of them hotrodders like all the time hangs out at Pops Zybysko's down the way."

His crochety eye told me he indeed thought I resembled a hotrodder or some other suspicious sort, but I wadded up the paper and trundled out, not giving a tinker's hoot whether he thought I was the ghost of Jimmy Dean descended to haunt his fan societies.

I squealed my tires at his curb and managed to cascade water upon his windows, just for the hell of it. By twenty past nine I had bumped across the railroad tracks into the Millwood area and was encased in a corner public telephone cell, getting in my call to Industrial Flats. F. X. Magruder came on the wire, harrumphing and hollering for whoever it was to speak up, he damned well had a meeting—

"Havoc, F. X. I'll expect to do financial business today because I'll have the goods by noon."

"Bringing them here?" he chortled. "Why, I thought you'd probably be in a cell at the police station. You had quite a soiree at your apartment last night, didn't you? Heh-heh." I clutched the un-read newssheet in my pocket as he continued. "But listen here. How about arranging for transmittal of a copy to those rascals in South Bend? If you've really turned the trick, you seamy little crook, I want to move on it immediately."

"Providing you keep your part of the bargain about no prosecution for Willis."

"By God, I may be a rat when it comes to the competition, but the solemn word of Thomas F. X. Magruder—"

"Swell, swell," I interrupted. "Collect your scientific hordes because I plan to bring along the gentleman who will forward the bogus to Rx. When I place him—and the copy—in your hands, I expect a check placed in mine, after which I'm going to try and straighten out certain difficulties with a constabulary and my rental agents."

"Ten thousand dollars can straighten out quite a few difficulties," he chuckled.

"Let us fervently hope and pray. Be seeing you, F. X."

So saying, I hung up the horn and rapidly dialed the number of the last vital link in the chain, Gray B. Ainslee.

"Why, little partner!" he cooed in a mellow manner. "I have been up and in my best gray flannel suit since six this morning. Are we about to cement our partnership?"

"We are. Can you get hold of a car and park it in front of the Lincoln Heights Branch Library by ten or a little

after? I'd prefer to use your car. We're going out to UPI and
get the phony document rigged immediately, and my vehicle,
ah, might be slightly warm in that general vicinity. The
library, I mean. How about it? Can you make it at ten?"

"Less time than that, partner of mine. I'm not far from
Lincoln Heights right now." His tone grew lower, more coy.
"Tell me, old buddy, that library isn't the place where—"

"The full account afterwards. Just plant yourself according
to instructions. What's your car?"

"A little old white Thunderbird. It'll be there."

"If it isn't, you're going to lose your hard-won reward,"
I growled, hoping to menace him from indolence into rapid
action.

"Farewell, old partner."

I crawled in the car and formed the mental opinion that I
was going slightly nutty from all the alarms I'd suffered during
the last twenty-four hours. I expected FitzHugh Goodpasture's squads to come raining from the heavens in para-
chutes, and Candy Cain's crowd to materialize in puffs of
smoke with their rods spitting. The Millwood street lay quiet.
Only Ainslee and Connie Willis knew approximately where
I was. The deal was almost closed. A ten thousand dollar
bonus loomed before sundown. Whistling jauntily, I at last
unfolded the morning rag I'd bought in the tobacco shop,
and even its gloomy lead story couldn't unnerve me.

The bannerline article dealt with an alleged riot occurring
the preceding evening in a flat belonging to one J. Havoc,
unemployed, in which riot Detective First Grade FitzHugh
Goodpasture and two assistants had mixed it up with two
dozen—that was Goodpasture trying to make it large for
the Chief Inspector—armed hoodlums.

Goodpasture and his pair of comrades had suffered severe
injuries about the face and head, but the worthy bull was
still at his desk that morning, directing the search for the
unsavory Havoc fellow. The most disheartening item in the
whole account was the statement that but three of the gunsels
had been taken into custody. The remainder had fled from
the building during the confusion.

Which meant that Candy Cain had a large force still

extant. Stuffing the paper under the seat of the auto, I
vowed to see what I could do to take Cain out of circulation
and stick him with the Hunter-Magruder homicide rap,
immediately upon leaving UPI. I might take lumps myself
from Goodpasture and his staff, but they might also tend to
be lenient in return for a tip about the genuine culprits.
Stool-pigeoning that way struck me as kind of second-rate
ending after all my grand dreams of repaying Jalasca, Sparks
and associates for the way they handled me outside The Ego,
but on the other hand, I had positively had enough of this
particular escapade.

The sky had spread out an optimistic blue overhead by
the time I drove back to the vicinity of the tobacco shop and
parked. Hands in pockets and porkpie jauntily on my skull,
I set out down the avenue to the Lincoln Heights Branch,
intending to pick up my heap when Gray B. chauffeured me
back from Industrial Flats.

I was taunted with vulgar jeers by the several squads of
leather jackets lounging across the way at Pop Zybysko's
Sweete Shoppe, but they did not molest me otherwise. I
passed the Lincoln Heights Public Trade and Industrial
School, from behind whose wire-grilled windows several
agonizing screams sounded. Ah, the younger generation . . .

Still, absolutely nothing could spoil my mood right then,
not even trundling by the Hidden Charm Brassiere Works,
which seemed to be peaceful enough after my demolition
of yesterday. Crossing the alley behind the library, I noticed
a cheaply-garbed gent lounging against the wall, reading a
newspaper. I had a sudden start for fear he might be an
agent of the brassiere management posted outside in the
event of my return. That was a screwy notion. Dismissing it,
I approached the corner of the library fronting on the park,
halted and peeked around the corner in a circumspect manner.

Although a good dozen souls were sprinkled through the
greening expanse of the public playground across the way,
most reading newspapers or lounging on benches taking in
the warming air, one of them had the look of bulls. Further,
not a solitary vehicle appeared on the circular pavement

running around the park, save a public bus just cruising out
of sight on the far side and a neat white Thunderbird parked
directly before the imposing marble steps of the library.

Impulsively I stepped around the corner and began to
walk in the direction of the portal of the book joint. Striding
against the sun, I had difficulty making out Gray B. Ainslee
behind the Thunderbird's wheel. In fact he appeared strangely
unlike that manufacturer's representative.

A small dong-dong of alarm was set off way back in my
cranium, but somehow it did not succeed in slowing the response of my feet, which carried me forward greedily to the
Thunderbird and the pillars of the Lincoln Heights Branch.

Then my mind remarked upon a singular fact. Though
the morning was growing pleasanter by the moment, it had
drawn no females into the park. All the guys lounging upon
the benches and among the shrubbery were guys.

This remarkable revelation was followed by one of even
greater import. As if on signal, the persons in the park
began folding away their newspapers, rising from their
benches and unbuttoning their jackets. All seemed drawn
irresistibly by something in my vicinity. They strolled toward
the white Thunderbird. Once this penetrated my noggin, I
took another terrorized peer at the T-bird.

Where I thought I'd seen only Gray B. before, I saw
another party.

Both parties hurled themselves violently from the vehicle.
Gray B. leaped out upon the curb-side. The gent from the
wheel, whom I had not recognized, now became all too
recognizable.

"We've been waiting for you, you little rat," shrilled
Charles (Candy) Cain, dropping his hand into his side
pocket suggestively.

Amidst the other hammerheads converging through the
park opposite I sighted a gaudy view of Biscayne Bay,
immediately followed by a tall individual with a red neck.

"Ainslee, you doublecrosser!" I howled. "Did you throw
in with this creep? When? How?"

"Never you mind, little ex-partner," Ainslee replied with
an expansive smile. "Right now you'd best better get your

scrawny little legs a-moving and hop inside the good old library and bring forth the application. I gather it's in there. Else you wouldn't have goose-chased me all the way over here. Oh-ho, see there, Candy?" he added, chucking his new associate on the arm in a familiar manner. "He gave it away right then, didn't he? Havoc, you surely don't have much of a poker face for a party playing in such a large game."

"Quit the damned gassing," Candy responded angrily. "I've got enough scores to square with that little shrimp to keep a heater smoking for weeks. If I didn't stand to make a tidy profit I'd fry him where he stands."

Candy jerked a thumb to the pistol corps loitering awkwardly in the shrubbery just across the street. "See those boys, Havoc? Those are some of the bunch you led into that mess with the cops last night. They kind of itch to get their mitts on you. But like I said when we talked before, I want to do things in a legitimate way. Sensible, you know? No, keep your trap shut and listen. So I got 'em controlled. All nice and mannerly. You walk inside the library. You bring us out the paper. Maybe I'll call 'em off. Maybe you can get out of this with your head still screwed on."

"Better do like he says, little chum," advised Gray B., tipping his hat to a maid who strolled by without giving us a third glance. Lowering his voice, Gray B. barked in a gravelly fashion:

"Because if you don't, why, by God this city has not had a shooting take place a public spot like this for a long time, but that little old record's going to be busted, and you'll be the buster."

"Up the steps, midget," Cain croaked. "Bring out the goods. No stalling."

"We read in the papers about all the phones being out of service around these parts," Gray B. added reassuringly. "And my associate here advises me the local precinct is much too far away for you to walk, better'n a mile, even if you could get out. Which you can't. Not with good old Charlie's helpers hanging around the alley in back."

Boob Havoc, not to read the signs. Doubtless the creep

to the rear had also folded up his newspaper and was even now reaching toward his shoulder rig, just hoping.

"You sons of bitches have been doing all the talking—" I began hotly.

"Yeah?" Candy grinned with toothsome cruelty. "And you got anything smart to say?"

Caught. Hook, line and sucker. Guess who the sucker happened to be.

"Nothing except that I'd better go into the library."

I turned and marched up the steps and passed through the revolving doors while Candy Cain and Gray B. Ainslee shook hands upon the sunlit sidewalk at the foot of the marble stairs, congratulating themselves upon the trap which they had just sprung.

Sprung tight right around my own greedy throat.

Chapter 14

INSTITUTIONS OF CULTURE and knowledge were slightly unfamiliar ground to a hustler of my type. I crossed the vaulted marble lobby with a good deal of trepidation. No, cowardice would be a better term.

Yet I figured gloomily I had better get good and acquainted with the Lincoln Heights Branch, since it would undoubtedly serve as my place of burial unless I could cook up a way out. Which looked not only impossible but suicidal.

Large placards decorated the walls: PLEASE! QUIET! or SSSSH! I shuddered to conceive of the noise that might prevail should Candy Cain and his recruits decide upon an invasion with all their heaters a-going at once. I stared around among the reading tables and spotted not a single soul using the library facilities. That, at least, was some relief. Fewer bodies on my conscience.

Proceeding straight across the lobby and not glimpsing

Connie Willis anywhere, I approached an apparition seated on a stool behind the main desk. This vision, some what beyond her seventieth birthday, wore what appeared to be a winding sheet of black silk done up at the top with a fussy little starched collar. A menacing ball watch descended from one side of her broad-like bosom. A small round doodad was affixed to the other side. From this doodad a chain arose to link with her pince-nez glasses. Her nose could have made neat halves of a sirloin on a butcher's chopping block. A plasticized sign on the desk denoted her as Miss Rumford.

"Eh . . . good morning, Miss Rumford," remarked I, taking off my porkpie and attempting to look as though a dozen heaters were not awaiting me outdoors. "Could I speak with . . . I mean . . . I came here looking for . . ." Eaglebeak's marble eyes turned my plasma limp.

"Young man, speak up!" screamed Miss Rumford. "I have worked here forty-one years, ten of them as chief librarian, and I am quite familiar with all those persons who have library cards issued to them. You are not one of them. From the disarrayed appearance of your clothing I should doubt very much whether you could qualify to be one of them. We do not issue cards to just everyone. People of questionable association—"

"You don't know the half of it," I said miserably, eyeing the revolving doors.

"What's that? Young man, did you want a card or did you not?"

"Frankly, I wanted to see Miss Constance Willis. Does she happen to be around?"

Sweeping the pince-nez from her beak and hopping off the stool with a rustle of her weeds, Miss Rumford glared at me.

"Is this connected with library business? I will not tolerate shoddy young men annoying members of my staff during working hours."

"You old buzzard!" I cried in an extreme of emotion. "There are a dozen tough gentlemen surrounding this palace of culture right this very minute! And all of them will be

glad to blow my head off, and yours, if I fool around much
longer. Where's Connie?"

An unhappy, frightened, soft small voice suddenly spoke
from the stacks:

"Right here, Johnny."

She looked so good to me, sweatered and skirted and my
size even in high heels, that I wanted to muss her up a little
right in front of Miss Rumford. On the other hand, the way
she looked—lost, alarmed all of a sudden—made me stop
trying for doubtful humor. Unless I salvaged the situation
within a few moments, I'd be about as dead as the unread
classics on Miss Rumford's dusty shelves. I swallowed with
difficulty.

"Connie . . . did you hear a little bit of what I told
this . . . ah . . . lady?"

"Young man!" shrilled Miss Rumford, waving her arms
vaguely. "Did you mean to imply that some sort of armed
persons are loitering outside these premises?"

"Will you kindly shut your trap, lady? Connie and I have
to figure—"

"Shut my trap?" she returned apoplectically. "I most
certainly shall not. I am going to telephone the police
station . . ."

Out went her hand to the instrument.

". . . and have them send over a half dozen men to put
you and your lunatic stories where they belong. In jai . . ."

Blink, blink. Miss Rumford withdrew her hand from the
Bell machine.

"Oh," she said in somewhat less strident tones. "I forgot.
The storm. Well, harrumph. No matter. Miss Willis, is this
miniature maniac someone with whom you're famil—"

"Connie," I said across the line of gabble, "this is a real
mess. I'm sorry. But we can't stand around debating. First of
all, where's your brother?"

"Down in the catalogue room, eating the sweet rolls I
brought when I came to wor—"

"Brother?" cried Miss Rumford, throwing up her hands
and upsetting a stack of books on the desk. "Catalogue room?
Sweet rolls? God in Heaven! What is happening to me? Am I

going senile?" She staggered against the counter. "That must
be it. Old age at last . . ."
"Miss Rumford, for God's sake!" I gave her a shake of the
shoulders. "Will you get away from here for a second?
Look—do this—"
I nudged her not-so-gently from behind the desk.
"Go up front. Reassure yourself. Prove that I'm no maniac.
Look out the front door. See all the big, tough men. Hands in
the pockets. Guns, Miss Rumford. Go see. Go see the guns.
Go on, you old bi— Miss Rumford. Be a good old girl."
Pushing and nudging, I managed to set her sensible shoes
moving toward the revolving exit. On this journey she continued to mutter to herself in a bemused fashion, pulling off
her pince-nez, releasing them and letting the chain on the
doodad snap them up. If she hadn't gotten geriatric and soft-
skulled before I waltzed in, brother, she would be now.
"Connie," I explained, "outside are Candy Cain and that
Ainslee, the one who was supposed to transmit the phony
report to Rx. Unless I get the report out to them in a reasonable length of time, a small army of gun-slingers will come
through here like Tecumseh Sherman through the land of
the peaches. They want me. Or more appropriately, my blood,
for a number of reasons I won't explain now. But just a
second ago, standing here prattling to that old lady, I had an
idea. If I walk outside with the application, I'll probably be
burned on the spot. You too, most likely. And even old Miss
Rumford and Freddie. By the way, is there anyone else on
the premises?"
"No, just Miss Rumford and me," she said, wide-eyed and
shaking to beat hell. "A boy comes in at noon, but— Johnny,
can't you take the application to them, make the—"
"Uh-uh," I said, full of conviction. "They'd puncture me
and everyone else around, just because this Cain is a screwy
nut who has a hard time settling anything except by making
it a corpse. One way or another, everybody in the library
has to abandon ship—I mean, get out safely, which we can't
do as long as the damned park is so deserted. This idea—it's
screwy, but it might give enough cover to get you and Fred

out of here, and the old lady, too. Now I'll have to stall them a few more minutes."

"Mercy upon us!" howled Miss Rumford at the revolving doors.

She turned, took half a dozen faltering steps, snapped her pince-nez abstractedly and fainted cold away.

"Money," I panted feverishly. "Coin money."

I pulled out my pockets.

"Anything and everything you've got. This stunt worked once back in the twenties—a publicity man named Reichenbach—never mind. If I can only get the hell away for ten minutes . . ."

Connie Willis, baffled, pulled out a drawer in the desk and lifted forth a metal tray.

"I don't understand what you're trying to do, but there's plenty of change in here from the two-cent fines we collect on late books."

I nodded, dumping the tray upon the desk top and filling my pockets with coins until they sagged heavily. I seized Connie once more.

"Is there a place where you can barricade yourself for ten or fifteen minutes? Just . . ." I found a singularly discouraging lump in my gullet. ". . . just in case this shennanigan fails? Or works a minute too late, after Cain's gotten itchy and stormed the bulwarks?"

Taking my hand, Connie pulled me for a step or three, pointed down a secluded and dusty aisle-way at whose end I vaguely glimpsed an iron staircase descending underground.

"Down there in the catalogue room where Freddie's waiting." Her eyes showed luminous and round. "I have a key. I do the cataloguing."

Nodding, I indicated the prone Miss Rumford.

"Take her with you," I ordered, but sweetly. "Stack a few dozen books against the inside of the panel, just in case— but I mentioned that, didn't I? Let's proceed to another point. The most important. Namely, pretty, how can I squirm out of this joint using neither the front entrance nor the employees' back door?"

With a miserable sob of dismay, Connie Willis flung her-

self upon my shoulder and clutched me in a frenzy. Her
stout reserve of courage melted in seconds.

"Oh, Johnny! If—if—saving us depends—on—on getting
out another way, then you can't! This is an old building. Just
—just two exits. Oh, Lord, what are we going to do?" she
finished, collapsing upon me in a trembling bundle of frightened flesh.

What a perfect opportunity to exercise my libidinous urges.
Soothe her. Murmur to her. Plant big brother's kisses upon
her tear-salted lips. And then . . .

I blinked down into the warm tangle of her hair. What in
the name of Federal Bureau of Investigation was possessing
me? Here I stood, an army of nasty souls waiting outside to
perforate me with leaden particles, and what did I think
about? Sex, sex, sex.

Perhaps I was suffering a bizarre sort of shock.

Perhaps my small self had been so long without appro-
priate female companionship of corresponding less-than-
average size that I . . .

Ding-dong!

Oh, George, and I'd thought we were squashed!

"Connie!" I yanked her off my lapels and gave her shoulders a few shakes. "Connie, for God's sake, stop the tear-
ducts a second and pay attention. It doesn't have to be a
door! Hell, no! For anybody else it'd practically have to be
a door, but in the words of those crumbs outside, I'm a midget. Made for midget-dimensioned openings. Think!"

"Why, you're right." She blinked, dabbing at her lamps.
"I never thought of—"

"Then do it promptly," I urged, believing I heard, above
the terrorized moans of Miss Rumford supine upon the marble flooring, a coarse voice crying my name from the street.
Candy should be growing highly impatient, straining to release his corps of guns.

"In what used to be the coal cellar," Connie breathed,
screwing up her forehead in concentration. "I think there's an
old coal chute. The library's heated by a gas plant now. No
one uses the chute. But Johnny, if I remember, it's terribly
small."

"Where is it in relation to the employees' entrance?" I jingled my pennies pockets, seeing at last the desperate means of our dubious salvation. "If it's not too near—"

"At the other end of the building. Just around the corner from the alley."

I dragged her forward to the place where Miss Rumford had begun to recover herself. Gaining her knees, waggling her head, she bubbled something about needing a good jolt of iron tonic to snap her out of this nightmare. While Connie conducted quick ministrations and assisted the crow to her feet, I pumped on to the revolving door, sucked a deep breath and batted through.

Down at the bottom of the marble stairs Candy Cain and the untrustworthy Gray B. glowered. Across the boulevard, Sparks, Jalasca and the other guns stood grouped in the shrubbery scowling at me like a bunch of prize fighters caught onstage during a performance of *Swan Lake.* I noted idly that one of the gun-hands had picked a flower and was sniffing it suspiciously, unaccustomed to working in such natural surroundings.

And the surroundings were natural right enough, just the way Mother N. had constructed them. Empty. On the far side of the oval park a pair of kids played with a colored ball. Otherwise my luck was horrible. Not a creature stirred anywhere.

"Where's the paper?" Candy queried, scowling. "You want we should come in there and start taking the place apart page by page? Look, wart! You've stalled long enough—"

"Willis is in there but he's locked himself in the catalogue room," I improvised, trying to appear as though I quaked with fear. It was not so difficult. "He won't come out. The door's four inches thick. Solid oak. I'm working on it. I just came out to tell you so you won't bring your cannons inside. I can see my spot. I'm all for breathing."

"You won't be doing that too much longer, little feller," called Gray. B. Ainslee with a winning salesman's grin. "Unless you trot that little ol' paper out here to us."

"Ten minutes," came Candy Cain's guttural pronouncement. "After that, the taxpayers are going to be faced with a re-decorating job. Re-plastering to cover up the slugs. Re-painting to clean up where we smear you all over the walls."

Flinging a whole bunch of peppermints into his mouth and crunching them maliciously, Candy shouted: "Any minute this vicinity is going to get crowded. We better have the papers before it does!"

Ten minutes?

Could I pull it off in ten minutes? My only salvation was a lack of excess fat to weigh me down and slow me up. Promising fervently to have the application on the steps in nine minutes and fifty-nine seconds, I whipped back through the revolving door, dogged to the side, bellied out on the marble and fumbled at the door's base, snapping a couple of door-stop locks into position.

It might not hold them long, but a moment saved was more breathing earned. Darting toward the desk, I found Connie holding up a shaken Miss Rumford. This person, her black silk covered with dust and her white dickie collar askew, was plucking absently at her pince-nez while she trundled along, cooing, "And a library always seemed such a nice, safe place to work . . ."

Down the stairs to the catalogue room. We managed to get Miss Rumford into its confines behind a heavy door which, though not four inches, was solid oak. I had a glimpse of a wispy-haired gentleman cringing in a corner of the chamber, watching through plate-glass lenses. A fat volume was crushed to the bosom of his suit in protective fashion. I closed the catalogue room door upon Connie, Miss Rumford and poor miserable Fred. But not before Connie's hand moved out and squeezed my wrist encouragingly.

"Please be awfully careful, Johnny," she whispered. "If anything happened to you because of what I've done—"

"Thanks a heap." I wore a silly grin and slammed the portal. Hearing the catalogue room door lock snick shut, hearing soft thumps as volumes one through six of *Britannica* were jammed against the wood inside, I started off at a trot down the basement hallway, following Connie's hasty directions. My pockets jingled and rang with coins.

How much time had elapsed already? Two minutes? Oh, murder.

Now why did I have to think of that word?

Beginning to breathe heavily, I opened a wooden door at the end of the cellar corridor and stepped through into dusty darkness.

Too late, I heard fateful noises above my head.

I let out a howl the instant a heavy object came crashing down upon my nut, turning on quite a few colored bulbs in my head and spreading me out prone upon some very cold, coal-dust-dusted concrete.

Chapter 15

FORTUNE SEEMED INDEED to be smiling at me with her full set of chinaware. That five-gallon paint container, probably unused since the Coolidge administration and stored precariously on a beam above the door, turned out to be empty. Though it knocked me down, it rendered me only half-conscious for perhaps thirty seconds. What did I care for the passage of time, la-la? This was all a vile fantasy, I'd wake in my own rack any moment now . . .

Instead I raised my head and perceived a chuffing gas furnace plant. Beyond it was a doorless cubicle I took to be the coal bin. Plunging forward, I reeled into this enclosure and noticed by my watch that approximately three minutes had now gone by. Would they wait ten? If they didn't . . . But enough.

The light in that joint was none of the best, filtering as it did through a pair of dirt-coated windows at ground level behind the furnace. It was sufficient, however, to help me make out a metallic square, well over my head up the wall of the bin. It looked to be a foot smaller than my shoulders. Those who had loaded coal into the cubicle in bygone days must have done so with an eyedropper. I gathered my legs under me, jumped high and caught the stone sill just beneath the chute aperture.

Hanging onto the sill with a single hand, firmly believing my arm would fall from its socket as a result of the strain upon it, I managed to get my other hand upwards and release the catch on the inside of the chute lid. Then I butted the plate with my head.

It squeaked, squealed and yowled in rusty complaint. Three more butts and it clanged open, flying upward.

I grunted feverishly and hurled my upper torso through the opening, forgetting for a moment that a hinged steel plate flying upward will also fly downward agin. It did just that, *whango*.

My suit lose several inches of cloth as I attempted to squeeze through the narrow opening while a vista of concrete sidewalk a few inches beneath my eyes swam in a dizzy fashion. I wormed, grunted, groaned, heaved my shoulders, and at last tumbled forth upon the cement just as the chute door closed again and gave me a good swipe on both my ankles.

Several dollars' worth of coins went jingling from my pockets. I tottered to a standing position and shoved as many handfuls as possible back my pockets. Blinking, I suddenly realized I was studying the business end of a rod.

"Thought you could sneak out, huh, you little meathead?" remarked the alley guard whom I had noticed reading a newspaper earlier that morning. "You might just as well of rung a whole bunch of bells, banging that chute thing around the way you did. Now, my orders—"

I gave him three dollars and seventeen cents' worth of change right in the map.

His weapon coughed, but I was moving.

The slug, though noisy, took hunks of stone from the library instead of hunks of cartilage from me. I gave him a belt in the shins with one of my loafers and a bust in the gut with my fist. He straightway released his grip upon the rod and clutched his midsection. Reversing his weapon, I hammered him upon the dome several times. Then I dumped him slumbering into the coal bin, pushing on the soles of his shoes and scraping him sorely before I realized he was considerably too large to make it through the aperture. Thus I left behind me the highly unusual sight of a pair of limp legs sticking from the library's wall.

I pelted off across the now empty alley, down behind The Hidden Charm Brassiere Works along the cross-alley, travelling in the general direction of the trade school and the Sweet Shoppe, my pockets jangling with money and the guard's equalizer tucked into the band of my trousers.

I covered nearly two blocks in less than a minute's time, keeping to the alley all the way.

I perceived ahead of me, bulking on my left, the pile of the public school building. I further recognized it from a group of young gentlemen assembled in the avenue through which I was running. These individuals, a dozen or so in number, formed a ring around an unfortunate who was backed against the wall in cringing posture. The lads, except for the victim, had zip pistols which appeared to be firing large construction nails, point first. The game seemed to be to discover which marksman could most closely graze the flesh of the unfortunate captive without bringing mortal injury.

As I skidded to a stop and dived for the green-painted rear entrance of the higher-learning palace several of the adolescent gangsters noticed me and took suggestive steps in my direction.

"Maybe he's a rutting juvenile officer," one of them remarked with a sneer.

"Hey, shorty!" another invited in a friendly fashion, "wanna play a real crazy game?"

"Another time," I cried, tearing open the door and darting through. But not before I had taken a handful of change from my pocket and flung it into the alley behind me.

In the tiled corridor to the institution, which ran straight forward to the street, only one bit of mayhem was taking place. This indicated that it was a quiet morning. A seamy youth wearing a hall monitor's badge was attempting to jam another of his mates, also be-badged, into one of the lockers lining the hallway. The second monitor, scrawny and under-sized, was resisting these attempts to have himself locked up alive. The attacker ceased and gave me a menacing glare as I raced by. The victim fell from the locker. Both youths forgot their grievances as I sprinkled fifty cents worth of small change upon the tiled flooring. I raced on toward the main doors calling, "There's more where that came from!"

I now gauged that I had approximately two and a half min-utes yet to go before Cain's troops stormed the fortress.

If they had done so already, growing hot-tempered and impatient, then I would have labored all for nothing. But I didn't dare stop now. In fact, I could not have halted had I desired, for I'd whipped up reaction behind me. The zip-nail squad had entered the hall, hot on my trail. The locker assassin had run to a classroom door and hollered:

"Hy, Lizard! Some fink just run through here throwing money away!"

This announcement, which I heard floating behind me, was followed by a stampede of feet.

"Pupils!" cried a forlorn and older voice. "Pupils, resume your places at once!"

"Ah, get out of my way, you old sheet!" came a merry cry, followed by a crash of furniture, a hapless scream and a renewed thunder of feet.

I plunged through the main entrance of the institution onto the sidewalk. And noted fleetingly that the classroom door had been ripped from its hinges as the entire population of the luckless instructor's class hurled themselves on the heels of the zip crew to see where the philanthropic fink had gone. Along the way a fight or two broke out as members of the mob scrambled for my thrown dimes, nickles and pennies. But the main body erupted in pursuit, determined that there were richer prizes to be had, if only they could capture the little shrimp racing ahead of them.

A bakery delivery van happened to be passing at the moment.

Heedless of this, I shot out between a brace of parked hot-rods and straight across for the aggregation of older young mobsters assembled in front of Pops Zybysko's. The van driver cursed, hollered and brought his vehicle to a stop with a painful cry of the brake-shoes. By this time the inmates of the Lincoln .Heights Public Trade and Industrial School had swarmed upon the outer pavements. Rather than lose a precious moment, a crowd of them went straight up the steps through the open front of the delivery truck and out the other side.

The driver vanished from sight with a feeble shriek. The youths emerging a few paces behind me carried armfuls of bread loaves and paper cartons of sweet rolls, whose contents they devoured with wolfish glee or hurled with insulting remarks at the truculent bunch decorating Zybysko's doorstep. I now found myself in the midst of this collection of menacing figures, dwarfed by leather-jacketed shoulders and pomaded duck tails which gleamed high above my head.

"Watch who you're shovin', cube," growled a shovee between his teeth.

"Let's teach him not to mess around this neighborhood, Gutsy," cried a mate.

"Pennies from heaven!" I exclaimed.

I hammered the stomach of a youth blocking my way, while scattering assorted change with my free hand.

This lost me the center of attention, for which I was deliriously thankful. I went lurching off back toward the library while cries of amazement and wonder rose afresh behind me. Huffing and puffing, a mighty ache beginning to rise in my rib cage from all my exertion, I nevertheless pressed on with my legs pumping to beat hell, adding all the speed of which I was capable. The next several moments would tell the tale.

Behind me, all disputes over coins having been settled by a series of quick physical engagements, both winners and losers set off in a growing pack to see whether the mad philanthropist would dispense more bounty.

He did, at the intersection of the last block this side of the library, thereby picking up a gentleman walking a poodle, a woman pushing a baby carriage and a pair of bearded students emerging from an apartment doorway.

The matron with the pram dove for a quarter, got her fingers nipped by a poodle, but the students got the loot.

A howl of outrage went up from the mob charging along half a block to the rear. This dreadful mass of youthful humanity now boiled over the sidewalks and filled the street. An auto squealed to a stop at an intersection. The youths marched up its bumper, hood and roof and down the other side. Another handful of coinage glittered in the sun. The driver abandoned his auto to join the chase and was knocked aside by the matron with the baby wagon. She thrust the swaying vehicle ahead of her as she ran, using it as a ram to knock a human barricade out of her path while her unseen infant wailed pitifully within.

Apartment doors popped open with regularity. The crowd swelled to frightening proportions. Its bedlam could be heard a mile. I ran with my head screwed around, watching the pursuit and trusting to luck to guide my steps. I had to keep just short of the outstretched fingers of the youths in the forefront of the mob or the game was washed up.

"We'll get you yet, you rich bastard!" shouted a lad in the lead, turning on the steam and drawing closer. "Bet you got a hunnerd thousand dollars in bills hid away."

"It's some sort of political demonstration!" cried a female from an open apartment window as we passed. "A bolshivek mob. Clarence, somebody ought to go for the police!"

The youth closest to me began to pump his arms with fiendish swiftness, intent upon tackling me and taking all my imagined wealth for himself.

My fingers were nearly scraping the bottom of my pockets, digging up the last batch of coins. While occupied with this matter and still running with my head screwed back to keep track of the leaders of the pack yapping after me, I crashed into some soul, stumbled, flew on by sheer momentum and skidded along the frontal wall of The Hidden Charm Brassiere Works, locked in the accidental embrace of a burly party whose executive-type face I thought I recognized.

"Excuse me," I chirped, wriggling free, "but this is a cross-country race."

Then his face lighted in an unholy manner. "Why, you're the bastard who wrecked the joint yesterday! Oh, by God! When I get my hands on you—"

What would transpire in that event I never learned. The doors of the undergarment factory exploded outward. Teams C and D, as well as all others, flattened the hapless executive beneath them as they plunged to join the mob, smocks a-flying, voices shouting out shrilly, "Which one, which one? There's a dime, I saw a dime. It must be that millionaire you see on the television, the one gives all that cash away. Get him!"

Two slight modifications in the nature of the pursuit occurred at that instant.

For one, the thrust of the brassiere workers moving into the stampede from a right angle at the side slowed the ranks somewhat. A beefy forelady even pasted the greedy youth who had been my chief pursuer, dropping him in his tracks. I plunged more decisively into the lead, crossing the alley behind the library and hammering for the park as hard as I could go.

Then, to the rear, the inevitable rumor and exaggeration set in. Though I had just that moment exhausted my finances, casting down two final measly pennies, a voice shrilled out hysterically, "I just saw him throw a dollar bill!"

"I got one, I got one!" howled the female with the pram. "It's a five-spot!"

An excruciating cry of sheer greed arose from the throats of the two hundred-plus souls charging behind me. I sensed a renewed burst of exertion among their ranks.

At the corner I risked a look back, saw the pram woman in the lead, hat knocked over her glazed eye. Her tot, no longer complaining, clung to the front of the carriage at the point of my unholy army, its little sacque flying in the breeze like a pink banner. As far back as I could see, the thoroughfare was choked from sidewalk to sidewalk. With a cry of exultation, I lurched around the corner, took half a dozen steps and threw up my arms.

"Candy Cain, here I am!'

A dozen souls swung around, all of them grouped at the top of the library stairs in postures which indicated that they had been marching in a phalanx, out of patience at last, to drag me from the library and take care of me for good and all.

Sparks and Miami Joe Jalasca bumped and pushed to the front of the crew to assume crouching positions upon the steps.

Heaters came forth and winked in the sun.

Gray B. Ainslee ducked with arms above his head behind Candy Cain who had come trotting down the steps, a weapon in his own hammy fist, to take up a standing position directly behind Sparks and Jalasca.

The others among the hired group were unlimbering their cannons.

Cain threw a heap of peppermints into his spasmodically working jaw with one hand. He raised his mammoth rod with the other.

"Fry the little bastard where he stands!"

At that precise instant, raising a roar, its pink sacque banner flying valiantly from about the shoulders of its mascot perched precariously in the rolling babybuggy the whole plunging, running, screaming horde of Havoc's Irregulars rounded the corner onto the field of battle.

Chapter 16

WHAT TRANSPIRED DURING the next few moments was nothing short of organized lunacy.

With a defiant cry I pointed square at Cain and his followers and shouted, "I'm fresh out of ten dollar bills, but I personally guarantee they're loaded with 'em!"

"Nobody pulls a trigger!" wailed Candy fretfully. "Cripes —women! Little kids!"

"Inside the library, for God's sake!" piteously exclaimed Gray B. Ainslee, stumbling all over himself in an effort to untangle an escape route through the disorganized mobsters. He hammered at the revolving doors which he naturally found locked. By that time I had commenced mounting the steps, several dozen of the crowd behind me whipped into a fury and determined to strip the supposedly rich gunsels of their last thousand dollar bill.

These hired guns, blanching before the spectacle of common citizens converging upon them with wrath in their collective eyes, hurled aside their heaters and began to plunge off along an oblique path down the opposite side of the broad stairs. Fractions of the mob split off, howling for blood or financial remuneration or both, and the leading gunmen got only as far as the shrubbery across the bolevard when a flying squad of Trade School inmates cornered them and began to search them unceremoniously. Finding they had no bulging wallets as I had announced, the lads were stoked to heights of outrage and began to batter the thugs to oblivion.

I noticed the perambulator jane right in there among them, delivering lumps with her handbag. I swung fast. I had my own affairs to handle now.

All of the criminal assemblage save Cain, Ainslee and the ever-faithful Sparks and Jalasca had fled from the battleground. But these four still presented a problem. Cain in particular seemed worked into a revengeful fury. He gigged Sparks and Jalasca in the ribs, mouthing angry orders I could not hear above the howl of the crowd. But his meaning was transparent.

A bullet went *ka-chow* over my head and cut a hunk from one of the pillars decorating the front of the Lincoln Heights Branch. I suddenly found myself abandoned upon the steps. The mob was occupied on the sidewalk, pummeling the daylights out of the dozen professional rods unlucky enough to be slow runners. Jalasca, on his knees, triggered another blast while I went behind a pillar, unlimbering the weapon I'd snagged from the alley guard.

"We may not be able to get out of here," came Candy's frenzied cry, "but by Jesus we can cool that little crap-head before anybody takes us. He ain't got any gun."

I poked my head an my hand around the pillar and yanked the trigger.

Miami Joe Jalasca exclaimed fretfully and seized his knee-cap, falling over and rolling down the steps. Sparks stuck his neck out in my direction, astonished, took one look at his pal tumbling down the steps toward the mob, stood up and handed his weapon to Candy Cain.

Then, before his employer could comment, Edward Sparks launched out down the stairs at a full run.

I said, "This is for the Ego where you wounded mine," and delivered a well-aimed bullet to his left lower calf.

As he spilled on the sidewalk, he happened to notice a group of the Zybysko Sweete Shoppe faction standing idly by with no one left to beat up. M. Sparks covered his face and began to beg for mercy. To no avail.

Gray B. Ainslee, meantime, was cowering behind Candy Cain, peeking out to right and left, searching for a means of escape.

Sucking in a long breath, I dodged out from the pillar, weapon up.

"Throw it away, Candy. You can't get in the library and you can't get through that crowd."

"I'm going to kill you, you son of a bitch," he said, and suddenly I knew that he meant it.

Candy's hand blurred up. His trigger finger whitened. I jerked the trigger on my own gun but I knew it would be a fraction too late.

"Police!" came the voice of the hiding Gray B. Ainslee. In exclaiming, he straightened and gave Candy an accidental bump from behind. Candy's heater thundered.

I could feel the slug whisper by, a second before my own gun went off.

Candy howled, caught his chest and pitched over on the steps, leaving Gray B. alone and shivering.

I slung down the rod, turned and squinted across the sun-lit park.

Where it had been deserted earlier, now it was filling rapidly with souls pouring in from the streets around all points of the circle. Sunlight winked on black polished auto hoods nosing swiftly around toward the library, scattering members

of the mob before their massive chrome bumpers. Blinkers
revolved. Sirens complained. Voices rose in a bedlam remin-
iscent of the Roman games.

Blue parties boiled from the black autos, swinging sticks.
With a dispirited, exhausted sigh I wandered over and sat
down on a marble step next to the fallen Candy Cain. Up
near one of the pillars Gray B. Ainslee had succeeded in
passing out.

I peered under Candy Cain's coat. The wound was high
on his right shoulder, worse luck. Reaching into the groaning
Candy's pocket, I unearthed a pepperment and popped it between my jaws. Sitting on the steps, blinking in the sun, I
awaited Detective First Grade FitzHugh Goodpasture who,
with a squad of billy-swinging precinct uniforms, was slowly
working his way through the mob with me as his goal.

Chapter 17

WHILE G. WASHINGTON watched me from one side, A.
Lincoln surveyed me from the other. Both appeared to gaze
on me with extreme distaste, as though I were receiving no
better than I deserved.

This picturesque scene transpired later in the afternoon in
Detective Goodpasture's miserably functional cubicle at the
city's headquarters building. A uniformed mug stood guard
within the frosted glass door, arms folded menacingly across
his chest, while FitzHugh, his red and grizzled-topped face
screwed into wrinkles of sheer cruelty, checked off items on
a clipboard, declaiming them one by one in funeral tones.

"Assaulting an officer. Resisting arrest. Bringing public
humilation on an officer—"

"I want my lawyer," I remarked, having none but putting
both my shoes on his desk as though I did. "You can't con-

vince me there's a statute on the books that makes it criminal to cause you public humiliation. You're just making that up because I gave you the slip in the brassiere works. Why don't you cut it out, Goodpasture? I'm not the least worried."

"You're not, eh?" he growled, squinting at me.

The harder he squinted, the more nervous I became. Finally he swiped my shoes off the desk top with a bat of his hand. "Why, you trouble-making little hustler, you're scared right down to the bottom of your crooked little spine. Permit me to continue."

His pencil checked off points with a total lack of mercy. "Wrecking private property. Withholding evidence. Inciting a riot. Possession of illegal firearms. Firing same to the public detriment. Oh, there's lots, lots more," he added, grinning ghoulishly.

I'd been permitted a minute with Connie when the whole mob of us—me, Connie, Dr. Fred Willis, Cain, Ainslee, Jalasca, Sparks, several of Cain's hired guns, the lady with the perambulator who reportedly had given some officer a hernia, and poor Miss Rumford—had been driven to headquarters. Connie in turn should by now have telephoned Thomas F. X. Magruder to come collect his application, or at least try to collect it before the bulls impounded it as evidence. But I had scant hope that F. X.'s ten thousand smackers would do me much good once Goodpasture got to pressing that list of charges.

With another fiendish chuckle, Goodpasture drew my attention back to his recitation. "How's that sound for a starter, Havoc? Think we've got enough to fix you for a while?"

"That list is outrageous," I cried vehemently, adjusting my shoes again.

"Keep your insolent little feet off my desk!" he exclaimed, knocking my shoes to the side a second time. "I may be a public servant but you're no longer the public. You are a prisoner. The prisoner of the state. Now, and for an indefinite period to come."

"For cripe's sake, Goodpasture, I handed you Candy Cain,

didn't I? He's wanted for murdering Lorenzo Hunter and
Shirley Magruder in that county upstate."

Glowering Goodpasture cooed: "Pray enlighten me, oh
fountainhead of wisdom. Exactly how do we know that Cain
is guilty of murder? Cain has not admitted it, has he? Oh, no.
He's lying in the hospital, unconscious and badly shot. And
when he recovers, unless I miss my guess he'll have eight
thousand witnesses to swear he was playing mah-jongg the
night of the murder. All you've done, you meddling little rat,
is make damned sure Cain will be on his guard if and when he
recovers. Thereby making it impossible for my department,
the legally constituted investigators of crimes committed
within this city, to quietly dig for evidence to nail him. Your
messing and muddling have caused us to let a murderer
escape. This is one more little thing of which I'll make a
note."

Savagely FitzHugh pencilled further damning words on his
clipboard. The desk phone rang and he snatched it up.

"Goodpasture. Who the hell—"

A gulp glugged from his throat.

"Why, Commissioner! I'm sorry, I didn't mean— What?
Oh, yes, sir. I'm interrogating him right now. Yes, sir, I'd be
glad if you would drop in. I know how much adverse publicity he's given the department. Besides, I really think you
should see him. He's quite a specimen." This last disdainfully,
after which Goodpasture replied oozingly, "Yes, sir, Commissioner. We'll be expecting you."

He hung up and smirked. "Guess that settles your hash,
doesn't it, Havoc? You're not just dealing with a detective
first grade, you've got the commissioner after you." He hefted
this clipboard. "Oh, just wait until I show him this list I've
worked up."

I wondered idly whether I might be able to suicide from the
window before that eventuality occurred. Regrettably, Goodpasture's office space was situated on the first floor of the
headquarters building. Thinking of other avenues open to
me, all of them ending in self-destruction, I was unprepared

for the sudden opening of the door and the appearance of
another plainclothes detective, unfamiliar, who announced:
"Ainslee just talked."
Goodpasture put his clipboard on the desk, sadly.
"He did?"
"The story this little punk told us is apparently bona fide.
Appears Ainslee went asking at The French Quarter for
Havoc sometime last night. When, I'm not too sure. But
Cain's girl friend, that del Rio broad, got wind of it. Cain
trotted over. They went back to Ainslee's place. Drew up a
quick partnership. If Cain strung along, they'd swipe the application when Havoc turned it up, resell it to Rx Corpora-
tion at higher price than originally planned, then split the take.
This afternoon Ainslee maintains Cain forced him into it.
That's so much bull, doubtless. But he also mentioned—and
included in his sworn statement and I think he's telling the
truth—that Cain admitted to him last night that he had
burned Hunter and that girl. Which should give us enough of
a wedge, don't you think, once we get Candy on the witness
stand? Well, I got to run along, Fitz. I'm due back with
Ainslee. Just thought I'd let you know."
Bang went the door. FitzHugh Goodpasture spun in his
swivel chair, studying me gloomily. Then he slammed his fist
on the desk.
"Well, by God, even if you did hand over Cain, that doesn't
wipe out even one of these charges."
He pounded the clipboard ferociously, making so much
racket that he failed to hear the door open.
A cough.
Goodpasture spun with a squeak of his chair. His jaw hung
down dismally. He scrambled, trying to gain control of him-
self as a portly, white-haired bureaucrat tromped into the
cubicle.
"Sit down, Goodpasture," the commissioner growled.
"You're over-zealous."
Smiling pleasantly, the commissioner extended his hand.
"How do you do, Havoc? I wanted to meet you."
"The pleasure's mine," I responded feebly, convinced he

was torturing me with that comradely grin. Goodpasture snapped a lead pencil in half and said:

"Mr. Commissioner, I just can't understand why you even sully your hands with a common little hustler like Havoc. Just look at this run-down of charges I've prepared—"

"Goodpasture, kindly get some sort of control of yourself. I have a gentleman outside I want you to meet." He fixed the helpless detective with a stern eye. "This gentleman is an extremely good friend of mine. In fact, we play poker together once a week, and have done so for the past eighteen years. I hope you'll put that list in your circular file and manage, in the future, to refrain from outbursts of the kind you've just made."

"You have drugged me," I said in a mush-mouthed way. "I am in a hashish dream."

"Oh, the hell you are, you greedy little rascal!" cried a male voice. Into the chamber with a sinful grin on his bandit's face strode the commissioner's regular poker crony, Thomas F. X. Magruder.

With a muffled sob, Detective First Grade FitzHugh Goodpasture released the top sheet from his clipboard and began tearing it into small bits above the wastebasket. For a moment I expected G. Washington and A. Lincoln to sob right along with him.

Chapter 18

"IT'S SO THRILLINGLY romantic," blurted the Crudgeford, barring my path. "I love roses, especially red ones. Except that I'm frightfully allergic and—and—"

While she slipped an index finger under her nose, I brandished the bouquet in her vicinity.

"Then kindly stand back out of the way or I'll be forced to infect you."

The Crudgeford retired regretfully behind her door where the current episode of *Life's Sorrowful Street* was coming to an end. Whistling, I mounted to the landing and knocked relentlessly upon the panel.

No reply.

Twirling my porkpie upon one finger, I knocked again.

From somewhere inside I heard a muffled cry.

Anxiously I pressed against the portal, discovering it was open. Once inside the apartment, I stashed the flowers on an end table—I still had nine thousand, nine hundred and ninety dollars in my bank account after purchasing them—and surveyed the pleasant scene in the small dining alcove.

A white tablecloth, dinnerware and a few pieces of expensive silver gleamed in the light of twin candles. A Magnavox performed. Its red light glowed in the gathering gloom of early evening. I heard Flying Henry's vibes beat softly in the air. All swell, cozy and grand. A fitting welcome for the hero and so forth. But sans a chick named Constance.

From dim recesses further in the apartment came a muffled struggling sound.

I tossed aside my lid and trundled along the hallway. I opened the first door to which I came.

Then I recoiled out of politeness.

Then I stepped forward again for a better view once my evil nature got the better of me.

Attired in the scantest of underthings, trim Miss Willis was attempting to get herself within the confines of a foundation garment.

"Damn and blast," she murmured. "Oh, damnation. He'll be here—oh, hell!"

Stepping out of the hateful garment, she kicked it with one bare foot into a closet, still with her bra-bound back to me, fists on her plump and enticing hips. I coughed discreetly.

Connie Willis released a small howl of alarm. She whirled and ran blindly across the room, crashing herself against me, throwing us both backwards. Through a little judicious pulling and tugging on my part, we fell athwart the bed. I reclined peacefully upon the spread. Connie's torso pressed firmly

against mine. Putting my hands beneath my head and smirking in an evil way I remarked:

"Pardon me, pretty, but the door was open and I thought
you looked like a dish who might want to buy a few magazines. I'm working my way through unemployment."

Embarrassment was chased off her features by a warm,
gurgling laugh.

"Then you saw? Damn you, anyway. Dinner'll be burning
on the range. Now get out of here and let me dress. After all,
I owe you something for what you did to help Fred. Everything would have been ready right on schedule, except I'm
getting so blasted hippy any more. It's just awful!"

"No, it isn't," I remarked, daringly lifting one of my hands
and placing it on the sheer black stuff covering that portion of
her delicious flesh to which she referred. "It is fine. You are
not hippy. You are built absolutely right. Especially since you
stand five feet and in heels, already."

Craning upward a wee bit, I kissed her speculatively.
Whereupon she mashed my head onto the covers with a return engagement far from speculative.

We tussled briefly and pleasurably, during the course of
which manuevers her brassiere disappeared miraculously.

I remarked, "Whatever special goodies you were brewing
upon the burners, Miss Willis, let me name them as the foods
I prefer least."

"You are an immoral man, John Havoc," she replied with
a rather wicked grin.

"That I am, pretty. And a greedy one, also. Though my
greed for green has been temporarily relieved. I now feel a
kind of greed stealing over me requiring another kind of
relief."

One of her hands went a-moving, and *whisk!* the black
sheer things flew off in a soon-forgotten corner.

She placed her hands on my cheeks and kissed me violently.
I disengaged myself.

"Excuse me, Connie, but I'd better hang up my suit."

Her body gleamed softly from the bed as I prattled:

"Inflation and all, can't afford to buy a new suit every day."

"Is that all you ever think of?" she laughed softly. "Ever, ever?"

What else could I do but demonstrate that I could, with effort, keep my mind from cash for as long as a whole night?

That stove was a living mess to clean in the morning.

—THE END—

The Armchair Detective Library was created in affiliation with *The Armchair Detective* and The Mysterious Press with the aim of making available classic mystery fiction by the most respected authors in the field. Difficult to obtain in hardcover in the United States and often the first hardcover edition, the books in The Armchair Detective Library have been selected for their enduring significance.

JAK   Jakes, John,
           1932-

           Johnny Havoc.

$17.95

DATE			